Your Free Gift

I wanted to show my appreciation for supporting my work so I've put together a Bonus Chapter for you. . . but don't read it yet!

Just visit this link:

http://outerbanksbook3_freegift.gr8.com/

Thanks!

Phoebe T. Eggli

Part of the Outer Banks Baker Mystery Series
A Time to Live, and a Thyme for Murder!
QUARANTINE AREA QUARANTINE AREA
Phoebe T. Eggli

Dedicated to those who live and love!

It's what our world needs, more living in the moment,

enjoying the people and the experiences around us;

whatever they may be!

Table of Contents

Chapter 1

For once Melissa Maples' summer started out relatively uneventful. The last two summers had been chalk full of mystery and mayhem from the get-go. Two years ago, she walked into her own bakery with her beloved nephew Logan to discover the dead body of a rival baker. One year ago, Logan found the dead body of his girlfriend's grandfather on his first day of fishing at Oregon Inlet. Both deaths tied back to her and the bakery somehow and they spent the early part of both summers fighting to prove their innocence in both events.

This summer started out peaceful, for the most part. At least no dead bodies, so for Melissa, that was a huge plus in her book. Logan was back for his annual visit. Another visitor was in town this year though. Kristina Payne, Jason Payne's daughter, was staying with her dad for the summer before heading off to the University of North Carolina (UNC) – Wilmington in the fall. She surprised her dad by showing up at his house the first day of summer vacation. Apparently, she hitchhiked to town from Elizabeth City. That wasn't the only surprise for her father. Krissy sported an entirely new look Jason didn't necessarily approve of, but knew enough to realize there was nothing to be accomplished by yelling at an eighteen year old woman about her blue hair and nose piercing. Melissa hoped to forge a relationship with her boyfriend's daughter. It felt so strange to use the term "boyfriend" when she was 46 years old, but it was appropriate. However, the young woman had other ideas completely that did not align with the hopes of Melissa and Jason.

Kristina, or Krissy as she preferred to be called, was a troubled girl on the verge of womanhood. Despite the recent remarriage of her mother, she was not thrilled that dear old dad was seriously dating someone. Every effort to befriend the girl had been outright rebuffed. When Melissa offered her a job at the bakery to earn some money for college, Krissy rudely refused. Not to be deterred, Melissa arranged for her friend Cheryl to hire the girl at her own soup, salad, and sandwich shop across the street from the Kill Devil Delicacies bakery. Krissy never knew her father's girlfriend engineered the job opening, and that was perfectly fine with Melissa.

They tried biweekly dinners at Melissa's house, too. Although Logan and Jason enjoyed Mel's culinary expertise, Krissy made sure to let everyone know her disdain for anything deemed non-traditional. The middle-aged widow spent her life in the kitchen as a pastry chef. She was renowned for her artisan breads and even won the Outer Banks Regional Bake-Off two years ago. Gourmet French meals were also a specialty of hers. Of course, Logan preferred hamburgers and French fries like any teenager but after several summers with Aunt Mel, he found he started to enjoy the gourmet meals just as much. Krissy, however, would sit at the table without saying a word and not touching her food. After dinner, she would excuse herself and run to the closest fast food chain, as evidenced by the pile-up of wrappers in the passenger side of her father's truck. Melissa tried her hand at more traditional fare in an effort to appease the young woman, but nothing she did or cooked seemed to be satisfactory. Still, she held out hope that by the end of the summer she and Krissy could become friends.

Now in the middle of June, the group settled into a somewhat comfortable pattern of everyday life. Logan helped Melissa out at the bakery in the mornings and then spent his afternoons with his girlfriend, Emily once she arrived back in town with her family. The poor kid tried to befriend Krissy too, but the young woman didn't seem interested in making new friends, especially with anyone who thought Melissa was the best. Logan adored his aunt and could not tolerate Krissy's snide remarks under her breath about her. Emily really didn't appreciate the attitude Jason's daughter exuded towards a family she had grown to love and respect. However, everyone was determined to try their best for Jason's sake.

Life had been more disruptive over the last week. Krissy's no-good boyfriend, Derek McCallie, arrived in town. Needless to say, Jason was not thrilled. The boy reeked of trouble. A phone call to his ex-wife revealed the young man was not the epitome of what a nice southern young man should be, what with being kicked out of school in the middle of his senior year along with a growing arrest record. Krissy claimed he turned his life around complete with passing his GED exam and a new job with a moving company in town. Ever a sucker for a story of a reformed young person, Jason caved and didn't ban Krissy from seeing Derek. Melissa had a bad feeling about it and worried he would soon regret that decision.

Melissa's thoughts often returned to how to better her own relationship with Krissy. After dating Jason for almost two years, she considered her present and future to be with him. It would be nice to have his daughter's blessing. She pondered that very issue as she mixed up a few more recipes to refrigerate overnight in the back room of her bakery. She had even consulted her brother, John David, by phone earlier that day. Sadly, he did not have any helpful advice on how to win over an already grown woman who happened to be the daughter of her boyfriend. Meanwhile, Logan already left to join Emily's family for an early dinner and Jason was resting up for the night shift with his partner, Cory Bronson.

With her hands and arms covered in sweet-smelling flour she mixed and kneaded dough while her mind drifted to the latest story from her friend Cheryl about the misadventures of employing Jason's daughter in her soup and salad shop – Cheryl's Seaside Sundries. Apparently, the blue hair and nose piercing weren't the only adornments Krissy had obtained. Cheryl called earlier to say she saw a peek-a-boo tattoo in the small of her back as the girl bent over to pick up something that spilled on the floor. Her straight-laced cop father would not be impressed. Melissa had no plans to tell him either. Cheryl tried to figure out what the tattoo was, but when she leaned to get a closer look she accidently knocked over a container of salad on top of the poor girl's head. Melissa would've paid money to see that. According to Cheryl, it was quite humorous to see the horrified look on Krissy's face as spinach and walnuts clumped in her blue hair and balsamic vinaigrette dripped down her forehead and off her nose. Clearly, the young woman didn't appreciate the laughter that Cheryl could not contain.

Krissy ran off in a huff to change clothes with a few select words muttered under her breath. She'd commandeered her father's truck during her stay, and Melissa now better understood why she'd heard the tires squeal as the young woman sped away moments ago. Cheryl called her immediately after the episode. Her friend could barely get the story out in between fits of laughter.

After putting away the pans of dough in the large refrigerator, Melissa came out to the front of her bakery. Her assistant, Maddie, had everything well in hand. It was an unusually quiet afternoon in the bakery for the middle of the tourist season. Pouring herself another cup of coffee, Melissa sat down for a few moments to rest while absentmindedly listening to the local North Carolina coast news on a small television in the corner of the bakery reception area. A young woman with too much red lipstick reported from the local hospital where there had been several cases of a strange nature. The symptoms were all similar – extreme fatigue, vomiting, losing consciousness – but the doctors were stumped. Over twenty new patients had been admitted to the hospital just that day with fifteen having been admitted overnight. "Oh dear," Maddie said softly, "Just what we need to scare off the tourists – a friggin' epidemic!" At that, Melissa rolled her eyes a little.

Maddie always made a mountain out of a mole hill. She suspected the same here.

As Melissa got back up to check on some rolls in the oven, she saw Jason's truck drive by way too fast for the small street. "Krissy's back," she thought to herself. She halted in her tracks as she heard the truck's brakes screech to an abrupt stop. A moment later, the quiet afternoon air was pierced with a horrifying scream. Without thinking, Melissa ran out the front door to the alleyway leading from the main street behind Cheryl's shop. She found Krissy on her knees in front of the truck, crying and screaming uncontrollably. Running over to the distraught teenager, Melissa put her arms around her asking if she was alright. Peering over her shoulder, she saw a horrific sight. Apparently, the truck had just missed slamming into poor elderly Mrs. Burnside whose body was lying in the middle of the back alley behind Cheryl's shop where she usually strolled to and from the shop and her home a couple blocks away.

The girl's screams continued, as Melissa yelled for someone to call 9-1-1 and she attempted to remove Krissy from the alley. Cheryl came out and led Krissy away as Melissa checked the woman's vital signs. Mrs. Ethel Burnside, an 82 year old sweet lady who frequented the bakery and Cheryl's shop, was unresponsive in a puddle of her own vomit. An ambulance was called immediately, but it was too late. The sweet woman was pronounced dead at the scene. The quaint seaside town of Kill Devil Hills, NC had its first casualty of the summer and a new mystery was born.

Chapter 2

It had been a tough night for everyone. Jason had worked until dawn as the Centers for Disease Control (CDC) had been called in by the governor of North Carolina to investigate the outbreak of illness in their small beach town. Of course, the mayor wanted his best and brightest detectives helping out the Feds. Krissy had been so distraught over nearly running over the already dead body of Mrs. Burnside that she had not argued about staying the night at Melissa's cottage.

As the sun peeked over the Atlantic Ocean, Melissa sipped her second cup of coffee as she relaxed on the back deck as the two teenagers still slept. Sleep eluded her most of the night as she realized her dreams of a peaceful, uneventful summer were dashed. Now, her beloved town may be in the death grips of a new and strange virus as well. With Mrs. Burnside dead and many others in the hospital, Melissa felt a twisting in her gut that this was just the beginning of another mystery. "Why couldn't they have just one normal summer?" she asked herself.

A soft knock on the front door came around 5:30 AM. Standing at her door was an exhausted Jason. Worry was etched in the frown lines of his forehead. He had not wanted to leave his daughter that evening, but knew she was in good hands with Melissa and Logan. She hugged him tightly. No words were needed between them. They had only been together two years, but they already had the kind of relationship where sometimes they didn't even need to speak to know what was on each other's heart and mind. This was one of those times.

After several moments, Melissa withdrew from Jason's embrace long enough to close the door behind him. Hand in hand, they walked back out to the deck so they could converse without waking the slumbering kids. With a huge sigh, Jason settled down in the cushioned loveseat he bought for Melissa last summer. Her deck had been littered with single chairs. Unconsciously, she had held back from purchasing seating for two since she had never imagined she would cozy up with someone else after the death of her husband, Kevin, several years earlier. Jason noticed though. The loveseat purchase had been like a test to see if she was indeed ready to give her heart to someone again – to him. She accepted the gift, but it had taken her several weeks before it became her "go-to" chair when Jason was there. The middle-aged cop accepted that all things worthwhile took time, so he willingly waited, uncomplaining.

"So how's my little girl? Give you any trouble last night?" he finally asked in a weary tone. She assured him Krissy was fine. They spent the night watching corny Mystery Science Theater movies and generally tried to forget about the events of the day. Krissy had balked at the idea of needing a "babysitter", but thankfully had not put up too much of a fight. It was the one time in years that Jason had put his foot down when it came to his daughter. She was not going to be alone after discovering a dead body earlier that afternoon and that was final.

"Tell me, any connection between poor Ethel and all the folks sick in the hospital?" Melissa asked. She had been shocked when Jason couldn't get off work to be with his daughter because the CDC had been called in by the governor. The elderly woman had been up there in years, but she had been as spunky and feisty as someone half her age. No one believed she just keeled over from old age. If there was a nasty virus going around affecting the residents of Kill Devil Hills that may explain her sudden passing.

Jason replied, "We're still waiting on her autopsy report and the lab results from the patients in the hospital. Everyone's showing the same symptoms;

however, the severity of symptoms differs greatly. One young man is mostly recovered already, while poor little Angela Vega is nearly comatose. It's a mystery."

Just then Krissy poked her head out of the back door and ran out to her father. It was sweet to see the father and daughter embracing. "Dad, can we go home now?" Melissa intervened by asking if they wanted some breakfast before heading back out, but the young woman already returned to her previously stand-offish attitude. She tersely thanked Melissa for allowing her to stay the night, but was anxious to get home. A chuckle from the doorway indicated Logan was up too. As a teenager, he knew the truce called last night would be short-lived. Jason chose not to argue with his daughter. Thanking Melissa again, he kissed her on the cheek and the duo left. Logan couldn't resist rolling his eyes as the door closed behind them. He loved his aunt completely and knew Jason did too. He couldn't understand why Krissy threw up a wall around herself when it came to Melissa. Didn't she realize just how awesome his aunt really was?

After a quick breakfast of turkey bacon and clementines, the two set off for the bakery on foot. Logan knew better than to broach the subject of Krissy's attitude with his aunt, but he was reaching the end of his patience with Jason's daughter. Instead he shifted the conversation to the upcoming picnic with the Hawkins' family on Friday night. He wanted to surprise his girlfriend Emily by baking something for the event himself. He had helped out in the bakery and knew his way around the kitchen a bit, but he desperately wanted something that would be of his own creation.

As aunt and nephew brainstormed ideas, they rounded the corner to the main street through town. Both immediately stopped speaking and stood completely riveted in place at the sight before them. The entire block had been cordoned off with police tape with guards set up to keep everyone out. On the other side of the block, they could see news vans with large satellite dishes. However, it was the mini-army in HAZMAT suits that shocked them. There had to be at least 50 men and women – couldn't tell with the full body suits and helmets – roaming the streets with beeping machines and clear garbage bags.

Regaining her composure, Melissa approached one of the cops standing guard on the sidewalk. She didn't recognize him, so she assumed he belonged with the CDC or another agency. Since dating Jason, she knew all the cops up and down the Outer Banks of North Carolina. "Excuse me, sir," she began, "Can you tell me why the entire street is roped off? My bakery is just down the block. Will I be able to get there sometime today?" Not one for conversation apparently, he shook his head and pointed to another gentlemen just walking up behind her. The man was clad in a sharp looking business suit with flaming red hair and spectacles.

"May I help you, mam?" he asked politely as she blocked his path. Melissa repeated her question. He sadly replied that the entire area would be off limits for an indefinite period of time while they investigated the apparent outbreak in town. Without another word, he donned a HAZMAT suit handed to him by the guard and walked away.

Melissa and Logan stood there a few moments longer surveying the spectacle their town had become. Their tiny seaside town no longer looked inviting and bubbling in summer fun. It resembled something more out of a horror flick, or even the scene in the movie E.T. when Elliot's house was taken over by the Feds investigating the little creature from another world. As they turned to walk back home, Melissa's phone buzzed in her pocket. It was Cheryl, her friend and owner of the soup and sandwich shop across the street from the bakery. She sounded dismayed as she reported that she was at the hospital now with her husband, Ronnie. He now exhibited the same symptoms as the other patients. She was already scared for her husband, but the CDC representatives at the hospital were only making her more frightened. Melissa vowed to get there as soon as possible. Hanging up the phone, she filled Logan in on Ronnie's condition and the two briskly walked to the next block to hail a cab.

Chapter 3

The hospital was bursting at the seams with the recent onslaught of patients with symptoms suspicious of a viral outbreak not seen in the United States in decades. Two entire floors had been reserved just for those patients and CDC personnel. In order to get onto either floor, one had to cover themselves in yellow, bulky HAZMAT gear. No one was allowed off either floor without first being sprayed down with a chemical sanitizer and changed into fresh clothes. Since neither Melissa nor Logan were related to any of the suspect patients, they had to wait for Cheryl to come down to a special waiting room in the basement of the hospital.

Melissa had never seen her friend so pale and distraught. Cheryl had aged at least ten years overnight. She attempted a faint smile as she exited the elevator and saw Melissa. Her friend wasn't fooled though. She knew Cheryl was petrified for her husband. The three sat down at a small round table in the far corner of the room where a soda vending machine hummed loudly. Wiping a stray tear from her cheek, Cheryl told them all that she knew of the situation. Last night Ronnie started feeling queasy after dinner. Within minutes he was vomiting uncontrollably and so weak he could no longer stand on his own. The paramedics were so concerned about contracting whatever was causing everyone to be sick that they wouldn't even enter the house until the CDC arrived with sanitization equipment and more HAZMAT suits. To make matters worse, the CDC representative told her that morning that she couldn't go back to her own home because it was under quarantine. She couldn't even pick up fresh clothes or her toothbrush. Every patient exhibiting the same symptoms also had their homes or businesses shut down as well.

Melissa explained to her friend that the entire block where their businesses were located had also been quarantined by the CDC. These guys meant business. Cheryl laid her head down on the table in despair. Putting a comforting arm around her shoulders, Melissa vowed to bring her back some clothes, as well as toiletries and some decent food to help keep her strength up. "Whatever you need," she assured her friend, "I'll take care of it."

As Melissa and Logan left the hospital, they passed the same CDC representative they encountered earlier in town. Intrigued by all the high drama ensconcing their town, Logan approached the tall, slender man and introduced himself. "Sir," Logan began, "can you tell us anything about what is making everyone so sick? We have friends in there and no one is telling us anything." The gentleman was polite, but obviously in a rush to check on the patients in the hospital. He gave the quintessential "We, the CDC, cannot confirm or deny a viral or bacterial outbreak at this time. We promise to keep the public informed as much as possible. With that response, he hurried into the building.

Unsatisfied, Logan decided to seek out his buddy Tanner Wiggins to see if he could help him snoop around. Not the brightest bulb in the socket, Tanner had the access he needed and was always easy to talk into just about anything. Of course, Logan didn't want to worry his aunt so he excused himself on the premise of using the time to catch up with his surfing buddies since they couldn't go into the bakery that day. Melissa suspected something was up with her nephew, but was too engrossed in her own concerns for her friend to worry about him.

As Melissa went back to her own house to round up some clothes to fit Cheryl and some travel size toiletries, Logan called up Tanner to meet him at The Surf Shack in thirty minutes. Tanner was the son of the county coroner and a complete beach bum. It wouldn't take much convincing to get Tanner on board with his plan. He wanted a preview of the autopsy results on Mrs. Burnside. Then, if anyone else unfortunately died of the same thing, they could conclude whether there really was a disease incapacitating the local townsfolk or something else entirely. He had heard of outbreaks of diseases that had been considered eradicated reappearing in the Midwest, but never anything all the way out on the east coast. Almost as an afterthought, he called up Emily on his way to meet Tanner. She was the smartest person he knew, and she had confided to him earlier in the year that she hoped to pursue a career in medicine. He hoped she would research the symptoms so they could narrow down what they were dealing with. Logan wasn't happy people were getting so sick and he was less happy about the town being overrun by the CDC, but he loved a good mystery. Perhaps they could figure this out before the Feds did.

Emily readily agreed and went to work immediately. She even called up her father, Joey Hawkins, who worked for the State Department in Washington, DC. Perhaps he could light a fire under someone there to find out what the CDC knew already and wasn't telling anyone. Tanner was already waiting for Logan at The Surf Shack with a bag of Crab Chips and two sodas. Since last summer, he had stopped disguising beers as sodas. His dad had discovered a Yeti cooler with several such camouflaged cans and had not been amused. Tanner also spent the first part of the school year in an alcohol abuse prevention program that had scared the boy mostly straight. At least enough to not take unnecessary chances getting caught.

Logan unveiled his plan to Tanner who was not as keen on the idea as Logan had hoped. Apparently, Dr. Wiggins had his son on a lockdown after catching him going through bags of unclaimed personal belongings left at the morgue. He had only been looking for money, but it had been enough to infuriate his dad. As the boys discussed the strange goings on in the town, a radio blared from inside The Surf Shack with the familiar beep of the emergency broadcast system. The message following the beeps was downright frightful. The CDC representative, introduced by the mayor as Dr. Brian Nelson, explained that the entire town of Kill Devil Hills was under a federal quarantine until such time as the CDC could determine the cause of the outbreak, treat everyone infected, and until such time as they could conclude the town was free of the contagion. He instructed everyone to go about their daily business, but to limit exposure to anyone outside their own home and to completely avoid contact with anyone exhibiting symptoms of the disease – nausea, vomiting, and dizziness. As the camera zoomed in on the doctor's face, he sternly advised that medical attention be sought at the first sign of illness. "The governor has declared a state of emergency in Kill Devil Hills until this situation is resolved. Blockades will be set up around the perimeter of the city. No one, including tourists, can enter or leave the area until otherwise advised." The doctor concluded his speech by informing residents that anyone acquainted with the patients already in the hospital would be interviewed by CDC personnel within the next 24 hours. Logan and Tanner looked at each other incredulously. Both shocked to find their little town on a government-mandated lockdown.

Almost immediately after the broadcast, Logan's phone rang. It was his aunt's boyfriend, who also happened to be a local police detective. Logan and Melissa were needed at the precinct for questioning by the CDC. He couldn't relay any specifics to the young boy. However, he indicated that the Feds had a working theory of the origins of the outbreak. Based on the current list of patients in the hospital being treated, they all had eaten at Cheryl's Seaside Sundries in the last 72 hours. Seeing as Melissa's bakery provided all the breads for Cheryl's shop, both establishments were under intense scrutiny. Logan hurriedly said goodbye to Tanner and raced off towards the precinct just a few blocks away.

Chapter 4

Talk about a bad case of déjà vu! Logan and Melissa knew this scenario well. Early summer inside an interrogation room at the police precinct. This was a habit both wished to break. The small room was unbearably hot as it was the middle of June in the humid North Carolina Outer Banks and the air conditioning in the building was on the fritz. Portable fans placed throughout the building did little to offer respite from the heat.

The precinct waiting room was packed with friends and family members of those stricken by the "illness". Even though the CDC had no conclusive evidence it was indeed a disease that had broken out in their small town, they had to treat it as if it were. The break room had been turned into a medical post where everyone was evaluated by CDC representatives who performed physical examinations of everyone known to have been in contact with anyone admitted to the hospital. Peeking out the interview room door, Melissa saw Krissy being escorted to the break room for her check-up by a short, plump woman in her late thirties with dark blonde hair pulled back in a hair net and her hands covered by Latex gloves. From where she sat, Melissa couldn't see the young woman's face but imagined this was not the kind of summer vacation Krissy imagined when she came to stay with her father.

Both Melissa and Logan already had their check-ups, complete with vials of blood drawn and having to pee into a small cup. Normally, all this should have taken place in the hospital, but the CDC wished to keep the "well" from the "sick"; as separated as possible. Jason had even told her that Dr. Nelson had put a ban on visitors in the hospital. Even closest family members weren't being allowed to visit loved ones anymore. Not until this situation was resolved. Anyone else needing medical attention, other than for those specific symptoms, were being sent by ambulance to nearby Kitty Hawk. He had just escorted one poor woman and her husband to the tiny facility there when she had gone into labor. They barely made it before the baby made its first appearance. Jason was thrilled it had waited though. He had no desire to be the one to deliver a baby.

Just as Melisa was about to lose her patience waiting to be interviewed by the CDC, the tall, flame-haired Dr. Nelson entered the room and closed the door. A quick introduction, the doctor got right down to business. He explained that it appeared all the patients admitted to the hospital with the same symptoms had one thing in common – they ate at Cheryl's Seaside Sundries. Melissa didn't dare tell him that her boyfriend had already filled her in on that tidbit. Without glancing up at the two interviewees, Dr. Nelson continuously jotted notes down on his legal size notepad as they talked. Most of the questions were quite innocent – Have you eaten at Cheryl's in the past? Have you ever gotten sick from her food before? When was the last time you ate something from there? Are you experiencing any of the following symptoms? The line of questioning went on for several minutes with nothing notable to report. However, the questions became more centered on the bread items Melissa provided to Cheryl's business which were numerous. Melissa's bakery provided all the bread sticks, sandwich breads, and bread bowls for soups and salads to the small shop.

Thankfully, Jason interrupted after thirty minutes into the interview. The small amount of air that wafted into the muggy room felt like a cooling summer breeze off the ocean, but the effect lasted only a matter of seconds. With a clouded expression, he handed the doctor a manila file folder. Exiting the room, he flashed a smile of encouragement at his girlfriend and her nephew and propped the door open with a small trash can. Unfortunately, the doctor preferred the door to be closed and once again they were ensconced in stifling heat. Dr. Nelson took his time perusing the file while Melissa and Logan waited with sweat dripping down their faces. His eyes were hidden behind his wire-rimmed glasses, but Melissa could see his forehead crinkle in contemplation. Finally, he placed the folder down on the table and looked back across the table at the duo.

"Mrs. Maples," he began, "I just received a report regarding what specifically the afflicted patients ingested from Mrs. Lankford's little restaurant. It seems that 100% of the patients ordered soups served in bread bowls from your bakery. The CDC does not believe the outbreak is just a bad case of food poisoning due to the severity and the variability of the symptoms experienced by the patients. However, we will need to conduct a thorough investigation of your bakery and all the food items there. We have not found any known contagions yet in Mrs. Lankford's shop, but are still searching for anything viral, fungal, or bacterial that could have jump started this outbreak. I would appreciate your permission to allow my personnel into the Kill Devil Delicacies bakery to do the same analysis. However, please know that if permission is not given we will simply serve a search warrant in order to gain access to the premises."

Flabbergasted, Melissa sputtered, "Of course, please do whatever you have to do." Pleased, the doctor made a quick phone call from the antiquated landline on the table and then continued his interview. His questions mostly centered on where she obtained the ingredients for her breads, her cleaning and sanitization procedures, and who had access to anything in the process from mixing the ingredients to delivery of the final products. All her ingredients were organic and grown locally, including all herbs grown in her own garden at home. Only Melissa and Maddie ever participated in the mixing of ingredients and baking. Logan usually delivered the breads to Cheryl, but sometimes Krissy would take them over before starting work.

Melissa wished she hadn't been so forthcoming by the time the interview was over. Based on the answers she provided, Dr. Nelson decided to quarantine her home as well. She listened helplessly as he called for a team of CDC investigators to search her home and seal it up. They weren't even to be allowed back inside to get clothes or toothbrushes! This guy certainly was serious about his job, which was a good thing but Melissa wished he wasn't so overly vigilant. She didn't intend to spend the next few days or even weeks in the same clothes! Dr. Nelson tried to reassure her. He even informed her that her friend Cheryl had already been evicted from her home until such time as they could determine if it was safe. For the moment it appeared that Melissa and Logan were homeless.

Chapter 5

With it being the heart of vacation season in Kill Devil Hills, and tourists trapped in the town until the CDC said otherwise, there were no hotel rooms to be found for Melissa and Logan. In addition, Cheryl had been banned from her home as well while her home was investigated for contaminants or contagions that could have made it into the food supply. As they walked out of the police precinct, Logan remarked snidely, "What exactly are we supposed to do? Camp out at the beach?" to anyone who would listen.

Luckily, there was one thing Melissa had plenty of in Kill Devil Hills – friends. She was already on the phone with her assistant Maddie when Jason ran out after them. After calmly reassuring Maddie that everything would be fine but the bakery had to remain closed for the foreseeable future, she was just about to ask for a place to stay when Jason interrupted her. With Maddie on hold, he insisted that Melissa and Logan stay with him. "Maddie, I'll call you back," she said into the phone and ended the call. Then, to Jason, she said, "I'm not so sure that's a good idea." Logan, of course, thought it was the perfect solution and said as much. Why shouldn't his aunt's boyfriend let them crash at his place?

Jason knew the reason Melissa hesitated to accept his offer – Krissy. He looked into Melissa's big, beautiful hazel eyes and reached for her hands. "I promise. We will make this work. It may not be easy and we may be a little cramped in my two bedroom townhouse, but we will make this work for us." Melissa smiled up at him and nodded, but added that if the situation was too awkward for his daughter, they would find alternate arrangements. With that settled, Jason went back into the precinct to wait for his daughter's interview to finish while Melissa and Logan strolled to the corner market to grab some supplies – toothbrushes, toothpaste, shampoo, etc.

As expected, having house guests didn't sit well with Krissy. With the extra arrival of Cheryl Lankford, the young woman became even grumpier than usual. Jason gave up his room to the two ladies, while he camped out in the living room with Logan. The guests tried their best to make things easy on their hosts. Quite frankly, Jason enjoyed their company and enjoyed all the scrumptious food cooked up by having two fantastic chefs as roommates. Krissy, on the other hand, was less than enthusiastic and complained incessantly. Melissa tried her best to give the girl enough space, but the cramped quarters didn't help matters.

A week went by and still the CDC wouldn't allow them back into their homes or businesses. The news reported that no new cases had been diagnosed, but the cause of the outbreak still remained a mystery. Some patients had recovered, but not enough to be sent home. However, some patients worsened over the week. It was mostly the elderly and very young that had the hardest time. Watching the news one morning as Melissa cooked breakfast, Logan was saddened to see a reporter interviewing one of the older teenagers that sometimes hung out with Tanner at the beach – Kyle Vega. His sister was one of the patients that had taken a turn for the worse. She was now in a coma. The young man was obviously distraught, but the smiling reporter just kept asking him questions and shoving the microphone in his face. Krissy walked into the room and remarked about the horrid smell coming from the kitchen. It was Logan's favorite turkey bacon with a smoked gouda cheese and spinach omelet. He rolled his eyes since obviously she was just being her usual rude self. He thought it smelled fantastic! Krissy saw Kyle on the news and made a comment about "poor guy", but then left in a hurry without eating.

Since they couldn't go into work and weren't allowed back at home yet either, Melissa and Cheryl spent a lot of their spare time volunteering at the local soup kitchen or trying out new recipes in Jason's kitchen. Jason enjoyed being a test subject for all their new creations. Some worked out well – like the lemon pepper chicken orzo soup paired with a new version of Melissa's thyme bread with an assortment of five different cheeses. The gazpacho with a dash of citrus splash served with her infamous Sea Salt and Rosemary bread was a huge hit, too. However, the country vegetable soup with parsnips in lieu of carrots did not go well with the jalapeño cheddar bread at all. Most evenings Jason came home to find his entire kitchen covered in flour and dirty dishes. He didn't mind; however, it was a sore spot with his daughter.

Melissa really was trying to make inroads with the young woman. She knew it was important to Jason. He loved his daughter immensely and he loved Melissa. More than anything he wanted them to form a lasting friendship, ultimately because he intended to keep them both in his life for all his days. Melissa realized this and truly wanted to get to know the young woman, but obstinate teenagers could be difficult on normal days. If one didn't want to be your friend, it just wasn't going to happen. As the days staying at the townhouse drew on it became more and more apparent to Melissa that things may not pan out the way Jason hoped.

She and Cheryl discussed the situation at length as they cooked and baked the days away. Her friend didn't have any advice to give except to let events run their course. No one could force the young woman to like Melissa and she expected Krissy wasn't even giving her a chance because she wasn't her mom. It would take time for her to accept Melissa as a permanent person in her father's life, but eventually she would have to do just that – accept it. Sometimes though, Melissa wondered if she really was a "permanent" person in Jason's life. She had never imagined having a long-term relationship with anyone other than her late husband, Kevin. After two years with Jason, she couldn't envision life without him. However, she now knew, better than most, that nothing is ever guaranteed. If his daughter absolutely objected to Melissa being in his life, she preferred to exit sooner rather than later.

Dwelling on the subject made Melissa too serious for Cheryl's liking. As they worked side by side in the kitchen, Cheryl did the only thing she could conceive of to lighten the mood – she took a giant glob of thyme bread dough and smeared in down Melissa's face. Stunned, and rather disgusted as she accidently inhaled a twig of thyme, she fought back. Within minutes the kitchen and adjacent breakfast nook were covered in dough, flour, and herbs. There wasn't a clean spot to be seen. They were so busy throwing whatever ingredients they could get their hands on at each other while yelling bogus threats and laughing hysterically, they didn't hear Jason come into the house with the CDC representative, Dr. Nelson behind him.

The two men watched in amusement as neither woman realized they were no longer alone. It wasn't until a glob of dough missed Cheryl and sailed through the room to smack Dr. Nelson in the face that they became aware of the men's presence. Both middle-aged women stopped in mid-battle with childish guilty looks on their faces before they both busted out laughing uncontrollably. Jason smiled sheepishly at their antics, but he couldn't gage the doctor's reaction. After multiple apologies, the women started to clean up while Jason explained the doctor's presence. Melissa offered him a wet washcloth to wipe the sticky dough off his face as she listened to what he had to say.

Apparently, the CDC had been unable to diagnose the exact cause of the outbreak, if that was indeed what this was. All the patients had similar symptoms, but severity and tolerance were dependent upon the overall health of the patient before becoming ill.

Nothing in their investigation revealed a virus, fungus, bacteria or any known contagion that would have affected such a large number of people. Cheryl asked, "Does this mean the CDC is pulling out of town? Can we all go home now?" Sadly, the doctor shook his head.

He continued his story though. After ruling out viral, fungal, or bacterial contamination, he ordered more tests run on the bloodwork from the patients when they were initially hospitalized and compared it to new bloodwork. This time he requested tests for known poisons, chemicals, or drugs. "Oh dear," Melissa thought, "Not poison again." Last summer poor Mr. Hawkins had been thought to have been poisoned by her lemon sage bread. The women waited for Dr. Nelson to finish when Krissy and Logan walked back in. Both teenagers were aghast at the sight of the CDC doctor in the house, but Logan chuckled at the mess covering the kitchen as well as Melissa and Cheryl's clothes and person. He couldn't wait to hear what happened. The doctor continued to explain that one thing came back on every single patients' bloodwork – a relatively new street drug called X15. It had not been a virus that made everyone sick. Somehow they had all ingested the dangerous drug. Seeing as the commonality was still Cheryl's soup and salad shop and Melissa's bakery, the DEA was on its way to Kill Devil Hills to take up the investigation from that point. Considering the circumstances, everyone could start returning to their homes and the quarantine was lifted, but Melissa and Cheryl's residences and businesses remained closed under government order. Everyone was shocked by the news, of course. Melissa had a ton of questions for the doctor, but he didn't have anything further he could reveal to them. "Mam," he began, "Neither of you seem like the drug dealing types. We don't believe any of the victims willingly knew they were taking drugs, particularly the elderly woman that unfortunately passed away. However, I suggest you both cooperate fully with the DEA to resolve this mystery. They will need to find out who is peddling this junk and how it ended up connected to your businesses. This is serious stuff here. If you or any of your employees are found to be connected in any way to this drug, you or they could go away to prison for a very, very long time."

Melissa and Cheryl thanked the doctor for his warning, but assured him they knew nothing about drugs being dealt in Kill Devil Hills or anywhere for that matter. They agreed to cooperate fully. With that, the doctor said his farewells as he headed back to CDC headquarters in Atlanta to give them a full debrief on the situation. Melissa started to clean up the kitchen as Cheryl showered so she could visit her husband in the hospital. He had mostly recovered, but the CDC order had kept him hospitalized. Perhaps he could be released from the hospital now, but with her house still cordoned off for the DEA to investigate they had nowhere to go. Regardless, she had been away from Ronnie for too long and rushed to get to the hospital. Logan helped his aunt clean up the kitchen while Jason fired up the grill outside for hamburgers and hot dogs. Everyone was so busy, no one noticed Krissy sneak back out the front door and dash down the street on foot.

Chapter 6

With the town freed of the CDC-mandated quarantine, Logan decided to celebrate by meeting up with Tanner and a few friends at The Surf Shack after dinner. Apparently, the entire teenage population of Kill Devil Hills had the same idea as the beach was crowded. A full-fledge party had broken out with music blaring and impromptu bonfires up and down the beach. He was glad his Aunt Mel and Jason had not ventured out with him though as he was sure the cop would have had to make some arrests for disorderly conduct and open containers on a public beach, not to mention some obvious underage drinking. Logan spied Tanner's cooler suspiciously, but his friend assured him it only contained highly-caffeinated energy drinks and sodas.

As Tanner mingled with some female friends of his from high school, Logan looked around for any signs of his sweetheart, Emily. He texted her on the way to the beach, but she didn't know if she could get away. Her mom had invited a group of ladies from her summer Bunco club over and needed Emily to help out. However, after an hour of waiting Logan was rewarded when a thin arm reached around his waist in a tight hug. He knew it was Emily before he even turned around. He'd recognize that lilac-scented perfume anywhere!

Logan fished out a soda for Emily as she regaled him with her ingenuity in escaping the horror of Bunco. Tanner ran up – soaking wet as he had plunged into the waves on a dare to catch a fish with his bare hands. It was probably best that he failed to catch his prey as the shallow waters mostly teemed with baby sharks and jellyfish after the sun went down. They were laughing at how ridiculous he looked with a strand of seaweed tangled in his long blonde locks when Logan noticed Jason's daughter a few yards away at the edge of the parking lot for The Surf Shack. He had wondered where she had gotten off to when she didn't show back up for dinner, but had considered she just didn't want to hang out with them – once again.

Tanner noticed the direction of Logan's gaze. He had a not-so-secret crush on the blue-haired rebel girl. He envied his buddy having to live in the same house with her for the last week or so. What he would've done to catch a glimpse of her in her jammies?! He knew Logan was too much of good boy to sneak a picture of her for him, but the thought had crossed his mind often. However, both boys didn't like what they were witnessing right now. Krissy was in a heated argument with her boyfriend, Derek. Due to the noise from the party, they couldn't hear what was said, but the looks on their faces indicated they were not having a nice conversation about whether to listen to Bach or Beethoven.

Although Tanner would love nothing better than for Krissy to dump that dirt bag, he hated to see her so upset. "Perhaps she'll need a shoulder to cry on later," he thought with a sly grin. While the party raged around them, he watched the altercation a bit uneasily. Deciding he didn't like the look of things, Tanner excused himself from Logan and Emily in order to get a closer view of the action. By this point, Krissy had worked herself into a frenzy. Whatever the dude had done, she was beyond ticked off. The look on Derek's face was a mixture of fury and fear. Tanner tossed a soda can in the trash can at the edge of the parking lot – within a few feet of the arguing couple. Good thing too as Krissy shoved Derek in the chest with a finger, while he responded by raising his hand to slap her across the face. He didn't get his chance though as Tanner sprung to action and grabbed his arm. Logan noticed the commotion and ran over to help out. The two subdued Derek as Krissy continued to scream at him. The boys were too busy keeping Derek from going after the young woman, but Emily heard what Krissy was yelling at him. She nervously tried to calm Krissy, but ended up being shoved out of the way.

Finally, Derek had enough of being screamed at and stalked away, hurling insults at Krissy and her meddling friends as he went. As he disappeared out of sight, the young woman began to stomp off in the other direction, but Emily stopped her. Tanner escorted her back to the picnic table they recently vacated and offered her a soda in the hopes that she'd calm down and hang with them for a change. Reluctantly, Krissy joined the group but wasn't in a mood for talking. After a few awkward minutes of no one saying anything, Emily decided to push her luck by asking what the argument was about. She had an idea after what she heard Krissy screaming at Derek, but she wanted confirmation. Because if what she heard was correct, Derek was in a lot more hot water than just being the typical juvenile delinquent. She didn't want to see Jason's daughter caught up in the storm. Not that she particularly liked Krissy, but she cared deeply for Logan and those he loved – including his aunt and her boyfriend.

Krissy apparently didn't want to talk about it, but Emily was not about to let the topic drop. To encourage her to open up, she admitted overhearing some of what Krissy screamed at Derek. "Either you can tell us about it, or we can mention this altercation to your dad," Emily warned. Defeated, the story unfolded as the party continued around them.

Derek had an intensive juvenile arrest record back in Elizabeth City. Mostly the usual shenanigans of errant youth, but a couple more serious crimes – like drug possession and drug dealing. He left his home that summer after being kicked out by his mom who had enough of it. When he arrived in Kill Devil Hills, he swore to Krissy that he was clean and wanted to pursue a more honest lifestyle. He even got two jobs – one with a local moving company and another with a beach house cleaning service. She honestly thought he was trying to go straight. "Should've known better," Krissy muttered as she took a swig of cola.

It wasn't until the CDC doctor stopped by the house that evening that she pieced together what Derek had really been up to since arriving in town. Truthfully, she only suspected but it wasn't a far stretch to assume the boy had something to do with the arrival of the new street drug that made everyone sick. No one was ill before he showed up. However, she couldn't figure out how the drugs came to make normal people sick who obviously weren't the druggie types. She wanted to confront Derek in hopes of either (1) proving he was innocent and had not returned to the world of drugs; and (2) if he was involved, finding a way to make things right. Finding

Mrs. Burnside's body in a pool of vomit outside Cheryl's shop had changed something inside Krissy. She didn't want to believe her boyfriend had anything to do with the demise of the sweet old lady, intentionally or not. If he were involved though, she wanted him to answer for it. However, Derek had not confessed anything, but only repeatedly told her that there was more going on here than a few sick folks in the hospital. His nonchalant attitude enraged her which had led to the scream-fest.

The three friends sat staring at the blue-haired young woman in awe. Emily respected that Krissy wanted answers in the death of Mrs. Burnside and was willing to risk her relationship with her boyfriend. Logan didn't know how he was going to explain this to his aunt. Not only would they be caught up in another criminal investigation, but Krissy could be easily connected to the drugs through her connection to Derek. Tanner just thought he may have a chance with Krissy with Derek on his way out of the picture. However, all three agreed that they had to help find out what really happened, and if Derek was involved. They reassured Krissy that they were there for her and would work together to get to the bottom of this mystery.

Chapter 7

It didn't take Logan and Tanner long to formulate a plan. Emily wasn't so convinced it was the best plan, but went along with it. First, they wanted to determine if Mrs. Burnside did indeed die from ingesting the drug, X15. Then they would investigate how the drugs got into the old woman's system. No one in their right mind would believe the 82 year old woman was a druggie. Actually, none of the patients hospitalized for the same symptoms were known drug users either. If they could figure out how Mrs. Burnside was drugged, then they could apply that knowledge to the rest of the test cases.

The plan wasn't a brilliant one, but convenient. Tanner's father was the coroner and kept extensive paper files in his office. Despite it being the digital age, he insisted on hard copies to be maintained in his office. This made things easier because the boys wouldn't have to crack a passcode or anything to hack into the computer system. All they had to do was gain physical access to the paper files. Over the last couple years, Logan gained some expertise in lock-picking, so that helped a lot. The Kill Devil Hills morgue didn't have the most advanced security system either.

As a cover, Logan called his aunt to say he was staying with Tanner overnight. Tanner left his dad a message to say he was crashing at a friend's house. Emily, unfortunately, had to go home before midnight so the boys were on their own. Seeing as they were sticking their necks out for her, Krissy tagged along as a lookout. Her dad wouldn't expect her home until much later. As of yet, he failed to institute a curfew for his daughter.

The streets of Kill Devil Hills were quiet as the trio walked up Main Street towards the municipal building that housed the morgue. The party-goers had long ago dispersed from the beach, but there were a few stragglers still roaming the streets on their way home or looking for another party. At this late hour, no one should be in the building. Even the security guard, normally stationed in the foyer, had retreated to the break room in the back where he could watch late night television. Thankfully, he had left a side door unlocked and slightly ajar to get some fresh air into the building since the air conditioner had once again gone out.

Logan and Tanner gingerly made their way through the door and towards the back stairwell. They could hear Conan's opening monologue coming from the break room as they tiptoed down the steps to the basement which housed the morgue. Despite the failed air conditioning, the basement was chilly. Goosebumps broke out on Logan's arms, whether it was from the cold air or the creepy atmosphere of the darkened morgue, he couldn't tell.

Using the flashlight apps on their phones, they fumbled around until they found the file cabinet in the far corner next to the wall that housed the dead bodies. Fortunately, Kill Devil Hills wasn't the suspicious death capital of the state so the elongated mini-freezers were usually empty. Regardless, being inside the room where autopsies were performed added to the general feel of unease the boys experienced. Already on edge for trespassing – it wasn't breaking and entering since the side door to the building had been open – neither boy wanted to be in there any longer than absolutely necessary.

The sound of the file cabinet door sliding open was thunderous in the small room. The thick concrete walls reverberated the sound within the room. "Just hurry," Logan whispered, "This place gives me the heebie-jeebies." Tanner flicked through the folders and retrieved the file for Mrs. Ethel Burnside. The boys placed the file on the metal table in the middle of the room where autopsies were performed as they perused the folder. Neither had a clue what they were reading since it was in medical terminology and the coroner's writing was atrocious. "We don't have time to read the whole thing. Use your phone to snap pictures and we'll try to decode it later," Logan advised.

Just as Tanner was about to snap the last picture, Logan's phone buzzed with an urgent text message from Krissy. Tanner's father had just arrived and was already inside the building. Logan poked his head out the swinging doors and listened. There was only one way out of the basement. There was no way they would escape without being discovered by Dr. Wiggins. Thinking as fast as his scared mind could, Logan ducked back into the room. No hiding spots jumped out to him, except what he dreaded the most – the human-sized wall fridges that were intended for dead bodies.

He indicated his plan to Tanner by opening up one compartment and climbing in. "Oh no way," he heard Tanner whisper. Logan left the door open just a hair to allow oxygen in. Tanner didn't have time to come up with a Plan B. Logan heard the boy utter a couple choice words as he squirmed into the small drawer next to his own. Just in time, too. The doors to the room swung open and the lights turned on as Dr. Wiggins entered.

It wasn't difficult to see something was amiss. The man was Type A to the extreme and kept things orderly with everything in its place. What he saw in his "office" was not up to his standards. The open file cabinet door was the first indication. Even if he hadn't noticed that, the file folder laying on ground next to the vault was a definite giveaway. Dr. Wiggins' first instinct was to call for the security guard upstairs. After all, he was a forensic doctor; not a cop. He just turned back towards the door when he heard a sudden blaring of a familiar song. Normally, the doctor didn't listen to anything considered hip hop or rap. However, this particular tune - "Turn Down for What" – he recognized as the ringtone on his son's new iPhone. He threw open the body vault door where the sound emanated from to discover his wayward child desperately trying to shut off the phone. With a coy smile, Tanner simply said, "Hi, Dad."

To say Dr. Wiggins was incredibly unhappy to find his only son in the frigid locker used to store dead bodies would be the understatement of the century. He certainly wasn't prepared for the added surprise when Logan popped out of the neighboring drawer. He allowed the boys just enough time to exit their enclosures before letting into them about trespassing and being out that late at night. The boys stood there solemnly with their faces downcast, trying their best to look apologetic in the hopes the coroner wouldn't call for the security guard.

"What in the blazes are you two boys doing in here in the first place? Lose a bet or something?" Dr. Wiggins finally asked. Tanner started to reply but Logan sensed a lie beginning to form as the young man stammered around for something that might sound legit. Deciding against adding to their sins by lying to Tanner's dad, he piped up with the truth – well, just not the whole truth. However, he chose to keep the part about the pictures they took of the files out of the story.

"Son, you know those files are confidential," he scolded. "I can't even close out Mrs. Burnside's file because now the DEA is supposed to arrive in the morning. The family keeps asking for her body, but they've ordered that I keep it here until they conduct their own investigation." At that, both boys looked back to the wall where the dead bodies were stored with grossed out expressions. "Yes, she's still in there. Actually, if Logan had chosen the next compartment to his left he would've had a roommate." Dr. Wiggins enjoyed watching the boys squirm with that revelation.

"Dr. Wiggins," Logan began, "We are really sorry for snooping. We didn't break and enter. The side door was open. We just wanted to see if Mrs. Burnside died of the same thing that inflicted all the patients in the hospital." He continued to explain that the CDC representative indicated the working theory was that drugs were ingested by customers of Cheryl's restaurant so she and his aunt would be under suspicion. After the last couple years, he didn't want to have to go through the same ordeal again. He clarified that they just intended to be proactive to help out the investigation.

"Logan, leave the investigating to the investigators. Go enjoy your summer like a normal teenager." With a slight grin and a wink, he added, "You can even take lessons in being a lazy, no-good teen from Tanner here." In a more serious tone though, he added that he didn't believe Cheryl or Melissa had anything to do with a new drug racket in town, so they should have nothing to worry about. Tanner started to bring up Krissy's boyfriend being a not-so-former dealer in Elizabeth City, but Logan nudged him in the side to shut him up.

Dr. Wiggins decided against involving the security guard upstairs, but Tanner and Logan were to pay him back by returning during the daylight hours to scrub the room - and the body vaults – cleaning as payback.

If they performed satisfactorily this one chore once a week, he would consider not telling Logan's aunt or her cop boyfriend about the incident. Tanner, on the other hand, was grounded and made to hand over his cell phone right then and there. The teenager wasn't happy about the punishment, but at this point he had no bargaining capability.

As Dr. Wiggins escorted them out of the building, Logan happened to realize that the coroner was working strangely late hours so he asked him about it. "Well, if you must know Mr. Jones, I was lying in bed unable to sleep because of something that came back on the latest lab work from poor Mrs. Burnside. I wasn't sleeping anyway so I came in to retrieve my notes to see if I could figure it out." Unfortunately, the coroner was not about to fill them in on what disturbed him about the test results. Tanner got into the car with his dad, but Logan insisted on walking back to Jason's place. He knew Krissy was lurking somewhere nearby and they needed to brainstorm their next move.

Chapter 8

The next morning Melissa thought it odd when Logan appeared for breakfast. "Wasn't he spending the night with Tanner?" she thought. Regardless, she was happy he was there. Cheryl made coffee for the entire household of guests while Melissa whipped up some crepes with fresh strawberries and cream. The aroma filled the entire townhouse and even enticed the normally late-sleeper Krissy out of bed earlier than usual. With the bakery and Cheryl's shop closed down by the CDC, there hadn't been a big reason for the girl to hop out of bed early for work. She had relished the extra sleep and sometimes hadn't woken up before noon. Today, despite her late night, the young woman even seemed somewhat chipper. Probably the first time since Melissa, Cheryl, and Logan became guests there, Krissy actually smiled and said "Good morning" as she poured herself a tall cup of coffee. Even Jason appeared surprised by the new demeanor exhibited by his one and only child, but he knew better than to mention it.

Logan and Krissy took their crepes outside to the back patio as the adults continued their conversation in the cramped kitchen. Ronnie, Cheryl's husband, would likely be released the next day from the hospital. That was fantastic news, but the Lankford residence was still under a Federal lockdown now with the DEA expected to arrive later that morning. Cheryl was anxious to get back into her own home, as was Melissa. She worried about "overstaying" her welcome at Jason's house. Of course, he loved having his girlfriend living there but everyone was well aware that the entire situation did not sit well with his daughter. Melissa respected the young woman's feelings and thought it best she vacate before all good will was eroded between herself and Krissy. She loved Jason and realized she wanted a future with him. However, without his daughter's blessing, Melissa knew she would simply need to walk away. She and Krissy would never forge a friendship if the current state of affairs didn't change soon.

After breakfast, Cheryl decided to plan out a celebratory feast for when Ronnie was released from the hospital. She refused to add one more guest to Jason's tiny townhouse, so she already made preparations to rent out a beach condo for however long it took to get back into her house. Before moving out though, she intended to show her appreciation to her host with a scrumptious meal. Melissa offered to come with her to the market as soon as she finished cleaning up the kitchen. Refilling his travel mug with coffee, Jason took off to work to meet with his partner, Cory Bronson, and the lead DEA agent expected to arrive that morning. Melissa poked her head out the back door to let Logan and Krissy know where they would be and ask if they needed anything. She was surprised to find the two teenagers with their heads together and talking in soft tones. They definitely looked like they were conspiring together, but regarding what she couldn't imagine. It wasn't like they had been chummy all summer. They usually avoided each other. "Maybe things are turning around?" Melissa thought with a smile.

After everyone left, Logan pulled out his phone so he and Krissy could look over the pictures he took of Mrs. Burnside's autopsy report. Most of the reports he couldn't understand, but Krissy was able to decipher some items, despite Dr. Wiggins incredibly horrible writing. The elderly woman had died from drug overdose. That was blatantly clear, but the coroner couldn't determine exactly how she came to have drugs in her system. Krissy read off the chemicals found in the blood work, as well as from tissue samples. She wasn't a scientist, but easily identified those most commonly found in synthetic street drugs. Logan wasn't sure he wanted to know how she knew that information. Seeing the questioning look he gave her, Krissy admitted that she had taken Advanced Placement Chemistry in high school, passed the test for college credit, and part of the course allowed her the opportunity to conduct a research project alongside some graduate students from UNC. Her research had been used by the students to obtain a grant for more research on how to effectively counter the addictive effects of the drugs used on patients in rehabilitation. To say he was shocked was an understatement. He never suspected she was such a smart student with interests above and beyond just getting by. She certainly didn't act or dress the part. Logan was impressed.

Krissy brought out her laptop to research the chemical composition indicated in the coroner's notes. Her hunch was that it would match with the CDC representative's claim that X15 was found in the patients in the hospital. Her hunch was correct. Apparently, poor Mrs. Burnside took in a large amount of the drug. The question now was "How?" Ruling out the possibility that the elderly woman had a street drug addiction, the teen duo brainstormed other ways she may have come into contact with X15.

Seeing as everyone that became sick had eaten at Cheryl's Seaside Sundries, Krissy theorized that somehow X15 came into contact with the food there. They both agreed that Cheryl certainly wouldn't have knowingly put that stuff in her food. Aside from a glass of red wine every now and then, she was as straight-laced as they came. There were a couple other workers at the restaurant, aside from Krissy, but they weren't likely suspects either. With an apologetic, but questioning look from Logan, Krissy realized that out of everyone who worked for Cheryl that she would be the more likely suspect. She quickly reassured him that she didn't do drugs, she didn't deal drugs, and that she didn't support those that did do drugs. However, a sad look crossed her young features which didn't escape Logan's notice. Without having to ask, he knew – Derek.

Begrudgingly, Krissy filled Logan in on Derek's shenanigans over the last couple years. Part of that entailed doing a little time in juvenile hall for drug dealing. When he showed up in Kill Devil Hills, he promised Krissy that it was all behind him. She wanted to believe him desperately, but there was too much of a coincidence with his arrival and the recent appearance of X15 in the small seaside town. Even if he was involved, neither teen could figure out how X15 got into the food supply at Cheryl's restaurant. It was a theory to go on, but they needed more information. After last night, Krissy didn't think Derek was going to be too cooperative in that category. Even if he wasn't directly involved, chances are he knew someone that was involved.

While at the farmer's market, Melissa and Cheryl's discussion centered around one topic – how did everyone that became ill come into contact with a dangerous street drug? No one in their right mind would believe that even a small percentage of the patients consciously took the drug, if any. Cheryl was nervous because everyone that became sick, and even poor Mrs. Burnside, ate at her restaurant. According to the CDC doctor, her shop was the focal point of the investigation. Somehow X15 had infiltrated her business. That meant that someone had to bring it in. At no time in the past had she had problems with her employees and she certainly didn't suspect one or more of them developed a new hobby drug dealing. However, one thing did bother Cheryl. There was only one outlying factor that made this summer different from any other summer over the past five years – her newest employee, Krissy. Cheryl kept these thoughts to herself for now though. She didn't want to alarm her friend, especially since this was her boyfriend's daughter that may be up to no good. Instead, Cheryl vowed to herself to see what she could find out about the girl before bringing her suspicions to Melissa.

Chapter 9

When Jason entered the precinct he knew the DEA had already arrived. The place was swarmed with unfamiliar personnel who had taken over all the local cops' workstations. The uniformed police looked frustrated as they tried to accommodate the onslaught of Federal agents while still attending to their own business. The only Kill Devil Hills employee not looking put out was Jason's partner, Cory. The man was smiling like a giddy child in a candy store. The elder detective knew the younger man was not completely satisfied with the life of a small town police officer. It had been obvious from Day 1 that he had bigger dreams for his career. Jason just hoped Cory didn't use this particular case to make a name for himself at the expense of some really good townspeople – namely Cheryl.

Chief Monroe stood just outside his office looking perturbed. He had been on the force for so many years, he completely forgot he ever had a life as a civilian. However, the last few summers of amped up crime was taking its toll. Now, for the third year in a row, his police force faced a much more serious crime than underage drinking on the beach and petty theft. As soon as the CDC doctor had said the word, "street drug", he knew the small seaside town was in dire trouble. Sure, they had arrested punks dealing in the back alleys and beaches alike over the years. But X15 was not your average, run-of-the-mill drug. Although the Chief knew they needed the DEA to help root out this particular problem, he hated having his police department overrun by the Feds. They mostly complicated matters, in his humble opinion. "No," he thought grimly, "this summer was looking to be the worst in recent history for Kill Devil Hills.

As soon as he saw Jason, the chief motioned him over to his office. "Bring that partner of yours, too," he yelled across the squad room. He closed the office door behind them. "Gentlemen," he began, "I know that I don't have to remind either of you to cooperate fully with the Federal agents, but I did want to discuss some items with you before their lead agent arrives. Apparently, Agent Garland didn't feel the need to check in with us before heading over to Cheryl's restaurant first thing this morning. He just sent his minions to take everything over here in the meantime." The chief filled the two detectives in on what little he knew of the turn in the investigation. They already knew most of the situation. The CDC ruled that everyone became ill due to the street drug X15. Most had recovered and would be released from the hospital in the next day or two, except for a young girl who was comatose and her diagnosis was not good. No one knew how the drug got into everyone's systems or who even brought the stuff to town. Even the DEA didn't believe everyone hospitalized, and even the deceased Mrs. Burnside, were druggies.

The chief continued, "Jason, the one common denominator in all this is Cheryl Lankford's restaurant. I know your girlfriend is good friends with Cheryl. I hate to do this, but I have to ask – can you remain objective in this case?" Jason assured him and Cory that he could. The chief didn't doubt it for a second, but his partner had a less than convinced expression. Regardless, Cory nodded his agreement. "Great!" the chief continued. "You two will be working side by side Agent Garland once he sees fit to honor us lowly locals with his presence. Lucky for you, that means you are the only ones in the station that actually get to keep your own desks and computers. Everyone else has been ordered to surrender their workstations to the Federal agents." It was highly apparent that the chief did not relish the idea of his police force being taken over by anyone. It had been bad enough with all the CDC agents swarming the conference rooms and halls. At least most of those guys had been doctors and nurses.

As they continued to discuss the case, there was a sharp rap on the office door. Without waiting for the chief to invite whoever in, the door opened and an incredibly tall man in his early thirties strolled through the door. Jason guessed this was Agent Garland. He had the look – athletic build, short-cropped hair, serious hazel eyes, and he exuded an air of confidence found only in highly trained military personnel. Glancing sideways at this partner, Jason noticed that Cory sat up straighter in his chair and his facial expression was somber. Either the younger detective was intimidated by the agent or desperately wanted to impress him.

The agent held out his hand while he introduced himself to the assembled trio. His name was Agent Thomas Garland with the Drug Enforcement Agency (DEA). Jason refrained from making a comment that they knew what DEA stood for. He didn't believe the agent would be amused. He asked to be called Agent Garland in front of the rest of the officers outside, but since they would be working closely together they could refer to him as Tom or Thomas. Chief Monroe, in turn, introduced himself and his lead detectives. As everyone stood to shake hands, Agent Garland moved around to the chief's side of the desk and took a seat.

Agent Garland didn't waste any time getting to the point. X15 was a highly dangerous street drug new to the scene. However, this was the first time they had seen a case of the drug anywhere outside of a major urban area. Currently, Baltimore and the streets of the nation's capital were in an X15 crisis. The drug had a high fatality rate when taken the usual ways – snorting or through a needle. The agent deemed Kill Devil Hills lucky that only one person died. He revealed he had already read all the medical reports on the patients in the hospital and the autopsy report on Mrs. Burnside. Due to the concentration of the drugs in their digestive system, and the main symptom being violent vomiting, the DEA believed that the drug had been ingested with food or drink. Since all reports of the victims did not indicate a high population of known drug users in the small town, they were going on the presumption that the drug had been accidentally consumed.

"Well, at least we are all on the same page regarding that point," Jason thought to himself. Agent Garland continued by explaining that the main issue was to find whoever introduced the drug to Kill Devil Hills and to find his/her suppliers. Since all the victims had one thing in common – Cheryl's Seaside Sundries – he planned to focus the investigation on the small shop, its employees, and its suppliers. At this, Cory looked over at his partner. This was not unnoticed by the agent who asked about it. Jason cringed when his own partner informed the agent that one such supplier was Jason's girlfriend, Melissa. He explained to the interested agent that the Kill Devil Delicacies provided Cheryl with all the breads she served with her soups, salads, and sandwiches. Not stopping there, even with warning looks from both the Chief and Jason, Cory went on to explain Melissa's mishaps over the last couple years with the death of her main competitor in her own bakery and the suspicious death of an elderly man last summer from poison that had been baked into a faux version of her artisan bread.

Of course, Agent Garland was highly intrigued with this information. Jason realized Cory thought he was doing his job, but he was still highly annoyed with the forthrightness of his partner. It wasn't as if Jason would hide that information from the agent, but did Cory have to make it sound so dubious? Chief Monroe started to explain the two situations, but the agent cut him off by simply asking for the case files so he could read about it himself. However, he delivered a stern warning to Jason – if at any time he believed Jason was withholding information or not doing his job properly in order to protect his girlfriend rather than find the culprit(s) with the drugs, then he would not only be off the case, but would also be issued a restraining order keeping him away from the investigation until its end. Jason nodded his assent. He had no intention of letting his personal feelings get in the way of the investigation, but he knew neither Cheryl nor Melissa had anything to do with the recent introduction of X15.

The agent seemed satisfied and proceeded with a quick review of what they knew and what they needed to find out ASAP. He notified them that he already sent uniformed officers to bring in all employees of Cheryl's Seaside Sundries for questioning. As if on cue, Jason looked at the office window to see his blue-haired daughter Krissy being escorted to an interview room.

Chapter 10

As Krissy sat alone in an interview room waiting to be questioned, Cheryl and the rest of her employees filed into the crowded waiting room. After a lot of discussion over the matter, Jason voluntarily recused himself from the questioning of his daughter. Not that the Federal agent would've acquiesced anyway. However, the elder detective requested that the young woman at least be given a lawyer or other adult to sit with her during the interrogation. After all, she was only eighteen. Not a minor anymore, but he doubted she had much experience being across the table from a sharp Federal agent asking her intimidating questions. Garland agreed, so Jason called in Janice Littleton. The young female attorney had been instrumental in protecting Melissa and Logan's civil rights when they ended up in the same interrogation room now occupied by his daughter. He trusted her implicitly, except perhaps her judgment in men. Janice currently dated Jason's partner, Cory.

Janice smiled at Jason and Cory as she walked into the bustling precinct. Jason readily smiled back, but Cory didn't. He kept his facial expression serious and barely acknowledged her. Jason guessed he didn't want the overbearing DEA agent to know his girlfriend was representing anyone who could be a suspect in the case. "What a jerk!" Jason muttered under his breath. Janice shrugged it off and proceeded to the interview room without the slightest sign of being perturbed.

While Cory seemed ambivalent towards the arrival of his girlfriend, Jason noticed Agent Garland had a much more positive reaction. His eyes grew a little wider and an actual smile crossed his face. Janice pretended not to notice or care about either man's reaction as she strolled into the interview room and shut the door behind her.

Krissy appeared nervous, but smiled when Janice entered the room. She'd met the woman at a cookout her father had in the early weeks of summer, before things got crazy. Although she would never admit it, Krissy admired the young lawyer immensely. They had conversed several times about a variety of topics, including whether she should pursue a medical or legal degree. Despite her rebel appearance, Krissy was highly intelligent. Janice had recognized that instantly as the young woman had cleverly argued about the recent legislation being considered in the North Carolina assembly regarding reforming welfare. Janice realized Krissy was actually ambitious and had dreams for her future. She just didn't want anyone to know. It may alter their perception of her. The attorney respected the woman's wishes for privacy regarding her intellect, but urged her to not be shy about her acumen and brainpower.

A few minutes later, Janice opened the door to allow the DEA agent and Cory into the room to begin the interview. Jason was surprised when, after just a couple minutes, Cory exited the room with a stunned expression. He came over to his desk muttering, "She kicked me out. She would rather deal with the Fed by himself. She actually kicked me out." Jason tried desperately not to laugh, but couldn't hide his smile.

Inside the interview room, things progressed somewhat smoothly. Agent Garland spoke in an authoritative, but softer tone than he used with the gentlemen. He didn't want to frighten the poor girl because he thought she would be the one most likely to provide any useful information. He already read the reports. She was the only new addition to Cheryl's staff that summer. Krissy was the anomaly in the equation. Therefore, she was a primary candidate for either being directly or indirectly involved. He didn't want her scared and clamming up. Besides, he secretly wished to portray his softer side in front of the pretty attorney. He knew it was unprofessional of him, but he had difficulty not staring into those gorgeous emerald green eyes.

They ticked through the usual simple questions quickly – name, age, employment, time in town, etc. He asked how Krissy liked working for Cheryl and if she made any friends on the staff. She responded in brief answers, sometimes with a look to Janice for approval to reply. Things appeared to be going smoothly until Agent Garland pulled out a manila file folder with Krissy's name on it. In it was a copy of her high school transcript, as well as write-ups from the principal and guidance counselors regarding her disruptive behavior. "It seems that your grades are phenomenal. Your SAT score is through the roof. You have numerous college recommendations from your teachers, but…some behavioral issues kept you in detention for twelve straight weeks along with a three-day suspension. I'm guessing these may have played into you not getting into a more prestigious university," the agent explained.

"Agent Garland," Janice began, "I don't see how my client's perceived issues in high school impact this particular investigation. Could you please keep the discussion relevant?" He assured her that it was relevant, so she requested he explain. In response, he pulled out another file folder from under Krissy's high school record.

"Miss Payne, do you know a person by the name of Derek McCallie?" he asked. Janice noticed the severe look that came over Krissy's face at the mention of that name. She didn't like where this was headed, but needed more information. Krissy nodded her head that she knew him. Agent Garland continued, "Are you aware Mr. McCallie has been in Kill Devil Hills this summer?" Again, she nodded in the affirmative. "Have you seen Mr. McCallie during your stay here?" Krissy started to explain, but Janice advised her to simply answer "yes or no".

"Miss Payne, how do you know Mr. McCallie?" he asked. Krissy explained they knew each other in high school and they briefly dated. The agent furthered his inquiry by asking about Krissy's encounters with Derek since he arrived in town. How often had they seen each other? Were they currently "dating"? When was the last time she had contact with him? Janice stopped the agent and requested a little alone time with her client before the interview continued. He readily agreed.

"Krissy, you need to be straight with me. Completely straight. Do you understand?" Janice asked after the agent exited the room. The poor girl nodded and explained the whole story to the attorney. She dated Derek until he was arrested for drugs in Elizabeth

City. He surprised her by showing up in Kill Devil Hills a few weeks ago and claimed to be on the straight and narrow path. He completed his GED for high school and took a job with a local moving company and a beach-house cleaning service to pay the bills. They had hung out since he came to town, but she wouldn't go so far as to say they were an item again. Janice could tell there was more Krissy wanted to get off her chest, but she was reluctant to do so. After some encouragement, the young woman confided that she questioned Derek herself when she found out it was drugs that had caused everyone to get so sick. They had argued because she didn't believe that he wasn't involved somehow. Most importantly, she had not seen or heard from him since their confrontation at the beach.

After advising the young woman to keep her answers short and to not volunteer any unsolicited information, Janice invited the agent back into the room. She found him in a deep discussion with two of his fellow DEA agents just outside the interview room. This time he sported a stern expression as he entered the room. "Miss Payne, are you or have you even been aware of Mr. McCallie being involved in drug possession of drug dealing?" By the look on his face, both women knew he already was well aware of the answer. Krissy tried explaining that Derek had promised her that he no longer used or dealt drugs, but a look from Janice shushed her. Agent Garland continued, "It appears that Mr. McCallie has resumed his illicit business since leaving juvenile hall a few weeks ago. He has an outstanding arrest warrant from Elizabeth City for distribution of the new street drug, X15. However, my team in coordination with the local police have been unable to locate Mr. McCallie. Miss Payne, it would benefit everyone involved if you could tell us where we can find your boyfriend."

Krissy sadly shook her head. She chided herself for not knowing better when Derek first arrived in town. Of course, he hadn't gone legit! Worse yet, she had no idea where he was now. Since their argument she had tried calling him numerous times to no avail. He didn't have a known address as he usually crashed at whatever buddy's house he could find on a nightly basis. He even told her that he sometimes stayed in vacant beach houses when he couldn't find a place. Krissy readily volunteered this information as the agent jotted down every single word.

Chapter 11

After a long ordeal at the police department, Krissy had to get away to clear her head. She knew she needed to talk to someone, but she wasn't exactly the trusting type. The thought of confiding in her own father that she dated a drug dealer and that he may be behind the recent rash of accidental overdoses and Mrs. Burnside's death frightened her. Although she put forth the persona of a carefree, independent, somewhat rebellious spirit, inside she deeply desired her father's love and approval. As she strolled down the street she found herself at The Surf Shack. The beach was crowded with summer vacationers and locals alike, but she felt immensely alone. Just her luck – as she walked over to a picnic table to sit down and relax she saw two familiar forms returning from the surf with their boogie boards – Logan and Tanner.

Logan sensed Krissy's tension as they strolled over to her. She never really smiled, but at the moment she sported an outright frown. He already knew she had been through questioning at the precinct earlier and was anxious to hear how the interview had gone. Both young men figured they were all in this together, especially after working together to break into the morgue after Krissy's argument with Derek. Tanner went inside and bought the group a round of orange sodas and bags of pretzels, hoping the blue-haired beauty would appreciate his laid-back gallantry.

Although Krissy had not felt like unburdening herself to a couple of teenage boys, she felt at ease enough with them to confide in them what transpired at the police station. Neither boy looked shocked about Derek coming to town to push drugs. It seemed to make sense that everyone started getting sick shortly after his arrival. Tanner tamped down his enthusiasm to pin the entire thing on Krissy's boyfriend. Sure, it would benefit him if Derek turned out to be a total loser and hauled off to jail while making him look more attractive, but he saw Krissy was hurting and didn't wish to make matters worse. "The thing is," Krissy said, "I think the DEA now thinks that I'm helping Derek. I swear that I thought he had gone straight. Otherwise, I never would have allowed him back into my life. If he is involved…" Her voice trailed off as if she didn't really want to finish that sentence. In her mind it was unimaginable that her boyfriend could be responsible for all this trouble and that he was most likely going to take her down with him.

"Ok, let me get this straight," Logan began. "Derek is now considered missing since the truth came out about the drugs being what made everyone sick?" Krissy nodded her head as affirmation. "Is there any chance, he ditched town? If so, isn't that problem solved?"

Krissy replied, "I don't think so. The DEA is intent on finding out how everyone came into contact with the drug and who had the drug in the first place. If they can't find Derek, they will probably still come after me." She put her face down on the table in dismay. She saw no way this played out in her favor. That good-for-nothing knucklehead was going to be the end of her hopes and dreams. Being mixed up in a drug scandal was sure to nix her college aspirations. UNC-Wilmington could easily revoke their scholarship and boot her out completely with that on her record.

Neither boy liked seeing the young woman so upset. Sure, they hadn't started off the best of friends. Krissy had been downright ugly to them at some points and Logan resented her rude treatment of his aunt, but no one deserved to go through this kind of pain. Trying to assure her, Logan and Tanner began to formulate a plan to help find Derek and clear Krissy of any wrongdoing. Although, in the back of Logan's mind he wasn't completely convinced she was entirely guiltless. It seemed a bit unrealistic that she had no idea her boyfriend was dealing X15 and that drug just happened to affect customers of Cheryl's Seaside Sundries where she worked.

The trio sat around for hours outside The Surf Shack concocting a plan to find Derek. He hadn't responded to any of Krissy's numerous calls and texts. That could be for a number of reasons, but she figured he simply didn't want to talk to her after their horrific argument. He knew how much she despised drugs and his involvement in the drug scene, so she believed he simply wanted to avoid her. He didn't have many friends in town that she knew of– only guys he worked with at the moving company, but Krissy admitted she probably just didn't know of his other "druggie" acquaintances.

Suddenly Tanner had a light bulb go off in his head and jumped up from the table, knocking over his soda in the process. "Dude! I got it!" he joyfully announced. "There's a huge party tonight over at the abandoned warehouse off Conway Avenue. It's supposed to be THE event of the summer. It's been hushed up because it's illegal of course, but that should be a prime location for druggie types to hang out, right? Maybe we can catch up with Mr. Bad News there or find someone who knows him and where he may be?"

They agreed it was definitely a viable alternative to sitting around waiting on Derek to magically reappear. However, they recognized they could get into big time trouble going to the party. Neither Logan's aunt nor Krissy's dad would approve. Actually they would probably outright forbid it. Despite hating the idea of lying to Aunt Mel, Logan agreed they had to do this covertly. Since Krissy was already on the cops' radar due to her known association with Derek and the fact that she worked at the restaurant where everyone became sick, they agreed that she should stay home to help cover for the boys' absence. Since Tanner knew the teens throwing the party, he could get Logan in. They planned to meet up at 11 p.m. at The Surf Shack and ride over to the warehouse with a couple of Tanner's stoner friends. Logan wasn't entirely comfortable with that idea, but knew they would need to blend into the party scene. What better way than to show up with known partiers?

Chapter 12

The plan to infiltrate the party worked like a charm. Tanner even gave Logan an impromptu lesson on how to walk and talk like a beach bum stoner. Logan wasn't comfortable in the role, but played his role well for a novice. There was a DJ blaring tunes from a makeshift stage at the front of the warehouse and beer kegs set up all around. Within minutes both boys smelled like stale beer as other party goers sloshed their drinks on them as they passed by. Logan inwardly cringed. He knew he would have to throw his clothes away before Aunt Mel got a whiff of them. As if that wasn't bad enough, the tell-tale odor of pot being smoked wafted around the enclosed warehouse. Yes, this was not Logan's scene. He desperately wanted to find Derek and get out of there before trouble ensued. Tanner shoved a red Dixie cup into his hand filled with the unmistakable amber liquid of beer. At first he tried to hand it back, but realized he needed something to blend into his surroundings.

The boys walked around aimlessly trying to not look like they were looking for someone. Logan was sure everyone there could tell he didn't belong. Tanner, on the other hand, knew a bunch of kids. There seemed to be two types of people at the party – beach-going surfer types and the more hard core partiers. Ages seemed to range from early twenties to preteens. Logan didn't want to know how the younger ones got into the party. As they made their way around the outskirts of the warehouse to scope out the scene, they passed by one tween female in a skimpy tube top and Daisy-duke shorts just as she turned towards the wall to vomit. "Yes," Logan thought, "this is lovely."

Tanner appeared to be having a good time as Logan struggled to pretend. It was all he could do not to bolt out the door. Suddenly, Tanner grabbed his arm and hurried towards the far right corner of the warehouse. "There's the dirt bag," he proclaimed. He was right. Just a few yards away was Derek McCallie, along with a couple other dudes that looked like they were up to no good. Tanner tried to get closer without revealing themselves so they could listen in on the conversation. He took out his phone, which he'd just gotten back from his father, to try to snap a picture to prove Derek was in town and who he was hanging with. At least they could prove he was still in Kill Devil Hills. Tanner held the phone down as if he is just hanging onto it, so as not to appear he's taking pictures. Both boys noticed one of the other guys hand something over to Derek in a small plastic bag as Derek handed back an envelope. Both boys nodded to each other and simply walked away from each other without another word. Logan realized he had just witnessed a drug deal going down. Both boys hoped Tanner caught that on his phone's camera.

They didn't have time to check the images captured as there was a loud commotion at the front of the warehouse. All they heard was "Cops!" being screamed as hundreds of teens and tweens tried to vacate the building without getting caught. In the melee, Logan thought he saw someone he knew escaping out the side exit. He couldn't be sure, but he thought it was Kyle Vega whose sister still remained in the hospital after becoming sick from X15. "Doesn't he work at the moving company with Derek?" he thought before Tanner grabbed Logan by the arm and hurried towards a window in the back of the building. Unfortunately, before they could climb through it to run off, a uniformed cop stood waiting just outside the window.

For more times than he cared to count, Logan was hauled off to the police station in the back of a cop car. Their plan worked – they found Derek, but the price was going to be high. He had no idea how he could explain this away to Aunt Mel and Jason. Neither boy wanted to get Krissy in trouble either, but their situation did not look good as they were escorted into the precinct along with a long line of other party-goers. Due to the small size of the police force, they had not been able to round up a lot of partiers, but Tanner and Logan had been caught. As he walked towards the back waiting room of the precinct, Logan passed by Jason's desk. Unfortunately, the detective was there working late that night. The shocked expression on Jason's face as he saw his girlfriend's nephew at that moment was a look Logan knew he would never forget.

Logan guessed his relationship with one of the lead detectives got him an early interview with the lead cop from Narcotics, as well as the lead DEA agent. He had been immediately separated from Tanner as soon as they entered the building. He hoped that Tanner used the same story he did, otherwise they would be in serious trouble. Logan knew it looked bad. It certainly smelled bad with beer and pot smoke stinking up his clothes, even though he didn't take even a small sip of the beverage and didn't dare touch pot or even cigarettes. After the usual questions to cover the basics – name, age, etc. the DEA agent took over the interview. He didn't get to ask his first question as Jason knocked on the door. He escorted in a visibly upset Melissa. Seeing as Logan was still a minor, she insisted on being present during his questioning. "I certainly would like answers to some questions myself," she stated with the closest thing

Logan had even seen to disappointment in his aunt's voice. Agent Garland agreed and the interview continued.

Logan tried to explain what had happened – that he and Tanner had gone to the warehouse in search of Derek McCallie because Krissy had been upset after finding out he was back to dealing drugs. The boys agreed to help her out and thought the party was as good a place as any to begin the search. "Let me get this straight," Agent Garland interrupted, "You, as a minor, went to an illegal party in search of a known drug dealer?" Logan realized just how bad that sounded, but had to nod 'yes'. His heart nearly broke when he saw Aunt Mel tense and close her eyes in dismay.

Not knowing what else to do, or that he should probably just shut his mouth and claim the Fifth Amendment, Logan continued. He told them how they did see Derek and they tried to get his picture with Tanner's phone, but didn't know if they got the image or not. "It certainly looked like a drug deal going down, but we weren't close enough to see for sure and we couldn't hear the conversation." Melissa, sitting beside Logan at the small table, groaned. Agent Garland sent the local cop back to the waiting area to find Tanner and his phone. Minutes later the interview became more crowded as Tanner arrived with his visibly annoyed father in tow. The phone was confiscated, much to the young man's dismay as he just got his phone back from his father. Agent Garland flipped through the images on the camera roll – mostly shots of the dirty floor and people's legs. However, there were two pictures that aroused his interest. One was still mostly legs but a small plastic bag was seen exchanging hands – just couldn't see the faces that belonged to the legs. The other image was a head shot of Derek as he turned to walk away after the exchange.

Agent Garland sent the boys off with the uniformed cop for blood tests for alcohol and drugs. Jason joined Melissa and Tanner's father in the room to discuss the situation with the agent. "Listen," Agent Garland addressed the group, "if their tests come back negative for alcohol and drugs, they can go home. We won't pursue charges for being at an illegal party. But…Tanner's phone is now going into police custody as evidence. This isn't enough to indict young Mr. McCallie for anything, and it's not enough to clear anyone else. As far as we are concerned, both Tanner and Logan put themselves in a very precarious position by attending that party. If it's true they only went to search for Derek to help out a friend, that's one thing. But there's nothing to prove they weren't just there for the party or to find drugs for themselves.

We are going to keep an eye on them even more so now – just so you are aware."

A short time later, both Logan and Tanner were returned to the interview room to await the results of their tests. Melissa crinkled her nose at the foul odor emanating from the teens. Tanner's father was beside himself at the trouble his son had gotten into. If he held to his threats, Tanner would be grounded until the end of time and find himself enrolled in a military institute come fall. Logan sensed Aunt Mel was holding back on what she really wanted to say to him. At this point, he knew he deserved whatever she had to dish out. He hadn't even considered what his dad was going to say when Melissa had to make that phone call.

A couple hours later, the boys were cleared to go home with no charges against them. Aunt Mel sternly led her nephew out the door without saying a word all the way back to Jason's house. However, Jason made it clear that as soon as he got off work later that night, they would all sit down for a nice, long chat to discuss this conundrum they were now all in.

Chapter 13

It was s somber group sitting around the kitchen table the next morning at Jason's house. Most had not slept at all. After the detective arrived home from work around 4 a.m., everyone was still up discussing the events of the evening. Logan was in hot water with his aunt for several reasons, but mainly for putting himself in such a dangerous situation. She had not called his father yet and was dreading that little chat. Krissy spent the hours a nervous wreck as she waited for her dad to get back home.

A weary Jason filled everyone in on what transpired at the police department after their departure. Melissa could tell something had him very upset and it was more than Logan getting busted at an illegal party. He kept looking over at his daughter with concern, but was reluctant to spill whatever news he was withholding. The raid last night rounded up several kids with drugs on them, as well as some intoxicated minors. The DEA had hoped to uncover someone with X15, but only found weed and a couple guys with some more high powered drugs. Jason related that Agent Garland was not happy about Logan and

Tanner's attempts to investigate on their own. However, he got the feeling that the agent suspected the boys' motives to go beyond finding Krissy's boyfriend. Without saying in so many words, he seemed to believe the boys were more interested in covering their tracks or helping someone cover their tracks. Additionally, with the victims becoming sick after eating at Cheryl's restaurant and Melissa's bakery being her bread supplier, the DEA seemed intent on focusing on the two women and anyone who worked with them or was related. Logan's little adventure last night did nothing to dispel that notion.

Krissy and Logan piped up at the same time trying to explain, but Jason wasn't interested. He scolded, "What you did last night was reckless and dangerous. Instead of helping, it did the exact opposite." He didn't elaborate concerning his own partner's comments to the DEA agent; about the last two summers when Melissa and Logan had been connected to Mrs. Stevenson's murder and Mr. Hawkins' suspicious death. Even though they had been found innocent of any wrongdoing in both cases, the situation didn't look good.

For a few moments the entire group sat in silence. The expression on Jason's face grew more anxious. His forehead was creased with worry lines and a vein bulged on the bridge of his nose. Melissa worried about what else there could possibly be making things worse. Jason took a deep breath and stared sorrowfully at his daughter across the table. Melissa's gut wrenched as she waited on Jason to speak.

Stretching his hand across the table to take Krissy's hand, Jason steeled himself to deliver his news. "Honey," he began, "there's something you need to know." Everyone stared at him as he paused. "The party wasn't the only issue we had to deal with last night. The reason I didn't get home until just now is that there was a murder last night. As uniformed officers scoured the neighborhoods and back alleys for stragglers from the party, or anyone that shouldn't be out that late that may be up to no good, a body was discovered in the alley behind the Kill Devil Delicacies." He glanced over at Melissa to see how she took the news that someone was found dead behind her bakery. The shock that came across her face broke his heart. Jason quickly refocused on Krissy though. That awful feeling in Melissa's gut clenched tighter at the ramifications of the news she now expected to hear. Grasping Krissy's hands in his own, Jason uttered the words he had been dreading to say to his daughter. "I'm sorry, Krissy. Derek is dead."

The young woman just stared at her father as if she didn't hear him. Melissa's heart broke for Krissy.

Even though Derek had proven to be a "bad egg", she realized the girl cared for him. Logan was speechless. As the news sank in, a single tear slid down Krissy's cheek. In an obvious effort to control her emotions, she stammered, "How?"

Jason had never held anything back from his daughter. He always thought honesty was the best policy, even if it hurt. Reluctantly he explained what he knew about the boy's death. Derek was found behind Melissa's bakery next to the industrial size garbage bin. Based on the condition of his clothes, it appeared he had been dumpster diving. There were bags of uneaten and half-eaten breads strewn around on the ground near him. Logan began to ask a question, but refrained after a quick look from Jason. The detective continued his story. They found a bag of a white, powdery substance they suspected to be X15 – probably the stuff Logan and Tanner witnessed Derek obtain at the party. It appeared that he had been stuffing the breads from the bakery with smaller bags of the drug. "Actually, the only leftovers breads with baggies stuffed inside them were your Thyme Bread Bowls," he said to Melissa. "All the others were tossed aside."

While all that information was interesting and strange, he still had not answered Krissy's question – How? Logan inquired if Derek had overdosed on the drugs, but received a quick shake of the head from Jason. Taking a deep breath, he continued. Early evidence suggested that Derek had been beaten so severely it resulted in death. It would be a day or two before the official coroner's report, but Dr. Wiggins was already on the case.

All color drained from Krissy's face as she comprehended everything she had been told. Derek was dead. Murdered. He had drugs on him at the time of his death and it was most likely the X15 drug connected to the recent rash of illnesses and Mrs. Burnside's death. Her boyfriend – the one who swore he no longer used or dealt drugs and said he had turned his life around – had been involved as she suspected. Now he had paid the price with his life. Despite all the lies, she still grieved for him. However, she admitted to herself that she was also mad as a hatter at him for the lies and for getting himself killed. Lots of emotions tugged at her heart as she processed everything. Finally caving in to grief, she wrenched herself away from her father and ran to her bedroom to cry.

Chapter 14

Krissy stayed in her room for the remainder of the morning. Jason and Melissa hoped she at least got some sleep, but doubted it. Although they both knew Derek McCallie had not been the most upstanding guy, they sought to understand the young woman's grief and tried to give her some space. Although exhausted, Jason took just a brief nap before returning to the police station. Before leaving he and Melissa discussed the ramifications of Derek being found behind her bakery business with the X15 drug stuffed into her own Thyme Bread Bowls. She promised to call Janice, her attorney, later that morning for advice.

Her phone rang around 10 a.m. as she sipped on yet another cup of coffee. At this rate of caffeine consumption, she'd be awake for the next week and a half. She smiled though when she saw it was Cheryl's number on the caller ID. Her friend had already moved herself out of Jason's place and into a beachside condo in anticipation of Ronnie being released from the hospital. They still weren't allowed back at their home while the DEA completed the investigation, so a condo would have to do for now. It was good to hear Cheryl's cheery voice on the other end of the line. If there was one thing Melissa needed now, it was her friend. She had called to discuss plans for a huge feast to celebrate Ronnie being released from the hospital later that day, but upon hearing the strain in Melissa's voice, Cheryl promised to be right over.

True to her word, the doorbell rang sooner than Melissa's mind considered possible. Yet, Cheryl even came bearing gifts in the form of cinnamon crumble coffee cake and a tropical fruit salad. The two friends retreated to the back patio to talk while the youngsters still slept. Melissa explained the horrific tale of Logan being hauled into the precinct after being caught at an illegal party, why he claimed to be there, as well as the news of Krissy's boyfriend. Cheryl sat in stunned silence for a few moments before simply muttering, "Oh dear". When she heard the details surrounding Derek's death, she shook her head in disbelief.

Jason called a little while later to remind Melissa to get in contact with her lawyer. From what he was hearing at the station, they were going to need Janice's assistance sooner rather than later. The tests on the powdery substance found with Derek was indeed X15. The DEA's working theory was that the drug had been stuffed into Melissa's bread bowls as a way to hide the drugs in transit. Somehow some of the tainted bread bowls had made it into the food supply at Cheryl's restaurant, either intentionally or not. Currently, forensics was running tests to see if the drugs leached from the bags into the actual bread before it was consumed. If so, what happened to the bags? No one reported finding flimsy bags of drugs in their food. Agent Garland and the DEA already completed their search of both Melissa and Cheryl's homes and found nothing, so that was good news. However, they were still investigating their businesses.

As soon as she hung up the phone with Jason, Melissa called her attorney. Just in time, too. As she was on the phone explaining the situation, there was a knock at the door. Melissa opened the door to find Agent Garland and two uniformed officers.

Everyone was escorted back to the police station for more questioning. It was clear that the DEA suspected Melissa and/or Cheryl knew more about the drugs in the food than they admitted. They answered all the agent's questions as best as they could. Thankfully, Janice was a top-notch attorney who didn't allow Federal officers to intimidate her or her clients. Melissa suspected from the expression on the lead DEA agent's face that he rather admired Janice's spunk and intelligence. He kept everything strictly professional, but she thought she noticed a sly smile here and there whenever her attorney said something brilliant or sarcastic.

The best Melissa could tell from the way the questioning went, the DEA believed Derek had been hiding the X15 drug in Melissa's bread bowls, particularly the Thyme Bread Bowls. All the other bread types seemed to have been left alone. Upon reviewing the customer receipts from Cheryl's Seaside Sundries, everyone that became ill ordered their meals with that particular bread. All the bread bags stuffed with the drug that were found with Derek were that type, while all the others had been left alone. Agent Garland contended that was the young man's way of keeping the drugged breads separate from the non-drugged ones. It was a simple system.

There were two main issues that now faced the DEA investigation: (1) Was anyone else involved in Derek's scheme (i.e., Krissy, Melissa, Cheryl, or anyone else employed at Cheryl's restaurant or Melissa's bakery); and (2) Who was responsible for the death of Derek McCallie? Based on all available information, Agent Garland reasoned that Logan and/or Tanner could also be involved since they had gone to such lengths to locate the young man for their friend Krissy. All this sounded preposterous to everyone but the DEA agents. Even the local cops had voiced their disbelief to their Federal counterparts. Janice urged their lead representative to listen to the Kill Devil Hills police on this matter. Derek may have been an unsavory character recently come to town, but the folks the DEA were targeting in their search were good and upstanding citizens.

Melissa looked out the small window of the interview room to see her one other employee, Maddie, being brought in for questioning. "Poor Maddie," she thought. "To think she took this job just to have something fun to do during her retirement. She certainly didn't count on being dragged into these circumstances." As she walked by, the elderly woman gave her a smile and a wink.

The DEA didn't have any evidence to hold anyone after initial questioning so they were released to go in the mid-afternoon. One thing had been made abundantly clear – the DEA had nothing but suspicions regarding everyone they hauled in that day. However, as far as Melissa was concerned, they were certain Derek was responsible for the accidental drug overdoses and Mrs. Burnside's death. They just needed to determine if someone helped him and if that someone killed him in the end.

Chapter 15

Later that evening, the somber group crowded into Cheryl's beachside condo to celebrate Ronnie's release from the hospital. Despite the ordeal he looked great. A little pale from his usual dark tanned self, but definitely in good spirits. He recounted how sick he had been and his experience seeing their other friends and some tourists in the hospital with the same symptoms. He was grateful almost everyone recovered so quickly, but lamented how sad it was that the little Vega girl had lapsed into a coma. The doctors weren't very optimistic at this point for her recovery.

After being at the police station most of the day, Cheryl's plan for a huge feast of homemade delicacies had been thrown out the window. Instead they ordered pizza and relaxed on the deck overlooking the ocean. Krissy was not in the mood to celebrate anything. No one blamed her either. In addition to her boyfriend being found dead in the wee hours of the morning, the DEA had questioned her the longest. She knew Agent Garland suspected she was aware of what Derek had been doing. At this point,

Krissy wouldn't blame them if they suspected she killed him too. Deciding she needed to be alone, she thanked Cheryl for the food and started to walk back home. Jason didn't think it was a good idea for her to be alone, but Melissa realized the poor girl needed some time to herself.

It was an early night as Melissa, Jason, and Logan returned home shortly after 9 p.m. Ronnie had tired easily after his whole ordeal and everyone needed some much deserved sleep. After everyone went off to their respective rooms, with Logan on the sofa, Krissy emerged quietly from her room. She motioned for Logan to join her on the back patio. Confused, he followed her outside.

Even in the pale moonlight that peeked through the clouds, he could tell Krissy was frightened. Without a word, she handed him a note on a shred of yellow lined paper. "I found this in my room when I got home," she informed him.

Logan read the brief note. Chills ran up his spine as his eyes scanned over the poorly scrawled words. "Your boyfriend was a scumbag and deserved what he got. Unless you keep your stupid mouth shut about anything you think you may know, you will end up just like him."

The young man read and re-read the short warning. What precisely was Krissy supposed to know that would earn her such a threat? When he asked her, she simply shook her head. She swore that she had not known Derek was back to dealing drugs until after everything happened. She didn't know his contacts or his friends, if he even had any. Her voice trembled and her hands were visibly shaking. Logan stood up to go get Jason. Her father needed to know Krissy was being threatened. He was a cop. He should be able to do something. However, she grabbed his arm to prevent him from taking another step.
"Krissy, we HAVE to tell your dad!" Logan insisted. "This is serious!" The young woman, however, was adamant to keep silent. She argued that by telling her dad, she was telling the cops. The note warned her to keep her mouth shut and she intended to do just that. The two teenagers brainstormed what they could do about the situation. Not only was the DEA on their case, but now someone apparently on the opposite side of the law had Krissy in their sights.

After a while, Logan decided to consult with Tanner. He didn't expect to get much insight from the beach bum with a heart of gold, but they needed another perspective. Krissy was against calling the other boy, but didn't stop Logan when he dialed the number. Tanner agreed to sneak out later to join them in Jason's backyard. Technically, he was still grounded until the end of time, but he was confident he could get out of the house. By the time he arrived, Krissy and Logan had exhausted all known possibilities about who would threaten her and why. However, Tanner had a theory. According to him, no drug dealer ever really worked alone. His supplier probably considered Derek's little girlfriend a liability to his operation in town. It was unclear by the note whether the person doing the warning was responsible for Derek's demise, but he wouldn't rule it out.

Logan still thought they should tell Jason about the note, but neither Krissy nor Tanner agreed. In fact, young Tanner was now intent on doing some detective work of his own. Inwardly, he hoped to win the gratitude of the blue-haired beauty. Unfortunately, he didn't realize the danger he would be placing himself in. No one else thought his plan was a good idea. Actually, the word Krissy used was "insane". Although hesitant to go along with it, Logan agreed in the end. Despite the adults already being fast asleep inside the house, the night was still young, so they put the plan into action immediately.

Tanner texted several of his former pals when he was still an official "stoner". He now mostly just pretended to be one, but had dabbled in the stuff briefly a year or two ago. After some back and forth with a dude named "Hoss", he found out what he needed to know. Several of the guys working for the same moving company as Derek were known to deal in this new drug fad, known as X15. They apparently were the only connections in town to get a hold of the stuff. Hoss and his crew tried breaking into the business but had received several beatings until they backed off and returned to just pushing pot. The small group was known to be ruthless and territorial. Even Hoss voiced his concern that Tanner should not associate with that particular group of thugs. No high was worth that.

Despite his friend's warning, along with Logan and Krissy's pleads to forget about it, Tanner took off claiming he just intended to scope the guys out. If things got hairy, he'd bolt. However, if he did find out anything useful then he could give the cops an anonymous tip. The bad guys would be arrested and Krissy would be safe. Logan thought his friend was taking this gallant hero act a bit too far, but there was no stopping Tanner when his mind was made up. After he left in search of the X15 pushers, Logan and Krissy kept a vigil on the back patio until they heard back from Tanner. Hours passed and they didn't hear back from their friend. As the sun started to rise and turn the sky varying shades of purple and then pink, Logan fretted that Tanner had gotten himself into trouble. Texts and calls went unreturned. By this point, Krissy had worn out a patch of grass from pacing and her nails were bitten down to nubs.

Deciding against waking up Jason or his aunt, Logan took off in search of his friend. Using the phone finder app, he tracked the young man down to an abandoned stretch of beach just southeast of The Surf Shack. What he found shocked and scared him. Tanner was stumbling around swapping at imaginary objects in the sky. From his rantings, it appeared the boy was seeing swarms of unusually large insects. There could be only one reason he was hallucinating – drugs. Logan ran over to him to calm him down. "Dude," Tanner slurred, "you got some industrial strength Raid or something? These bugs are HUGE!"

Although it was too early for anyone to be out on the beach except for the most dedicated sunrise watcher or surfer, Logan knew he had to get Tanner out of there quickly before someone reported seeing an intoxicated or high teenager roaming aimlessly. The last thing they needed was for the cops to discover him. The DEA could certainly use this situation to hammer the final nail in their case if Tanner was found with X15 in his system and Logan with him. Not knowing what else to do, Logan called his girlfriend Emily. Without explaining the full story, he begged her to drive out to the beach to pick them up.

Within minutes she was there in her mom's Lexus SVU.

After getting Tanner settled into his own bedroom and assuring himself that his friend was sleeping the whole thing off, Emily drove Logan back to Jason's house. She was less than thrilled he was out at that time of the morning and even less enthused that Tanner was in such a state. After promising to call her later that morning to explain the whole sordid story, Logan snuck around the back of the house to find Krissy waiting, half asleep with her head on the wrought iron table. Unfortunately, Aunt Mel exited the house just as he ran back up. Deciding it was time to be 100% honest, he told her everything. Krissy was horrified that Logan would confess all to his aunt. However, after hearing what transpired with Tanner, she begrudgingly agreed it was best.

Considering the severity of the situation, Melissa insisted that Krissy talk to her father as soon as he woke up. She promised the distraught young woman that they would all work together to keep her safe and to figure everything out. A short while later, Jason joined them on the back patio. Melissa and Logan went back inside to give father and daughter time to talk alone. In the meantime, she called Janice. The young attorney was certainly going to earn her wages this summer.

Chapter 16

As Krissy and her father had a good heart to heart talk later that morning, Melissa fielded a call from Agent Garland with good news for her. The DEA had wrapped up their investigation of her business and home. She was free to move back into her own house, and her bakery was now back in her control. He didn't reveal if the DEA found anything in either location to help with the investigation, but she assumed they didn't since she and Logan were innocent of any wrongdoing. As soon as she hung up the phone with the agent, she excitedly called Cheryl. Her friend had also spoken with the agent earlier that morning. She was cleared to move back into her own home too, but Cheryl's Seaside Sundries remained closed by government mandate.

The aroma of turkey bacon and cinnamon crepes brought Logan back to the kitchen. He had been on the phone with his dad for some time attempting to explain the situation. He left out a few important details like crashing an illegal party and getting hauled into the police station. Logan also failed to mention breaking into the morgue. That information could wait until Dad came out to visit next weekend, or never.

Looking around at everyone, it was evident to Melissa that they were all running on fumes. No one had slept more than a couple hours a night since this whole thing started. Jason sported more grey hairs, even in his beard stubble. Melissa found it added to his attractiveness. However, she made a mental note to check her own reflection for additional signs of grey. She wasn't ready to relinquish her light auburn locks to grey just yet, even if she was 46 years old.

It was a quiet group that convened around the small kitchen table. Melissa tried to lighten the mood by announcing that she and Logan could move back to her cottage and she could re-open the bakery. The only one that appeared happy about the news was Logan. After overcrowding Jason's tiny townhouse for quite some time, she figured he'd be ready to get rid of his guests. Even if he wasn't happy, she assumed Krissy would be gung-ho to get the place back to herself. However, both father and daughter seemed downright sad.

Melissa went on to explain that it would take a day or two to get the bakery back up and running, but she looked forward to getting back to work. With everything going on, and with Cheryl's restaurant still closed, she offered Krissy a job helping her out in the meantime. She knew Jason wouldn't want his daughter simply hanging out at home or the beach, especially now with the threatening note she received. Surprisingly, Krissy smiled and readily accepted the offer. They hadn't known each other long, but that was probably one of a mere handful of smiles she had ever received from the girl.

As Logan and Krissy cleaned up the kitchen after breakfast, Melissa and Jason retreated to the back patio with cups of coffee. He only had a few minutes before he needed to leave for work, but he was anxious to discuss the current situation. "You know that you don't have to leave so soon. I've really enjoyed having you and Logan here," he said while looking into her eyes. "Even Krissy seems to have adjusted well to your presence here." Melissa reassured him that she appreciated him opening his home to her and her nephew, but she really needed to be back in her own place. After being an independent woman these last few years, she rather craved her own space at times. However, she affirmed that it didn't mean she didn't love him and want to be with him. He shook his head in understanding and offered to help her move back in later that afternoon. Then a strange look came over him as if he just had a brilliant idea. "With the situation with Krissy, I really don't want to leave her alone at all until we find the creep threatening her," he stated. Melissa nodded in agreement. She didn't think it was a good idea either. That had been part of the reason she asked the young woman to work at the bakery with her until Cheryl could re-open her place. Unfortunately, that would still leave evening hours where the girl may be alone with Jason working. Then it hit her! She proposed the idea, even though she realized Jason already had the same thing in mind. Krissy would move in with her and Logan for the time being. She just hoped the young woman would agree. Strangely enough, when the idea was presented to her, she readily agreed. The threesome would move back to Melissa's that very morning.

With Melissa, Logan, and Krissy busy getting settled in at Melissa's cottage, Jason went back to the police station feeling a bit better about the situation. However, he knew he had to fill in his partner and Agent Garland about the threatening note and find a way to tell them about the X15 dealers that Tanner found without implicating the young man in anything nefarious. The boy had been wrong to seek out the dealers by himself, but he appreciated his courage in doing so. Logan had called Tanner just before Jason left the house to check on him. Although dealing with a nasty headache and severe nausea, he was okay. The young man explained that he ended up in that dreadful condition because the dealer had insisted on watching Tanner snort the drug to ensure he wasn't some snitch. He had spent the next few hours hallucinating different things – large bugs, glowing neon waves, and sand that tasted like sugar – before Logan found him. After all the young man had done to help out his daughter, he owed it to Tanner to try to mitigate the legal situation so he wasn't hauled in for doing drug use.

His partner, Cory, was waiting anxiously for him. Agent Garland had been asking for him all morning. The two detectives knocked on the Chief's door since the lead DEA agent had taken over his office. Surprisingly, Chief Monroe now ran the local police department out of a cubicle. The old man didn't appear to mind though. With everything that had happened in Kill Devil Hills over the last few summers, he was eyeing retirement. He'd a slight change of mind concerning all his 'professional guests', and decided letting the Feds take over suited him just fine.

DEA Agent Garland was on the phone but motioned them to come in and sit down. If possible, he seemed even grimmer than usual with his forehead creased in frown lines and dark circles under his eyes. Jason wondered if the man ever left the station to sleep. By the looks of him, he doubted it. Tersely ending the call, he looked across at the two detectives. "Fellows,

I've cleared Mrs. Maples to return to her home and business because we could not find anything else to connect her or her nephew to the case. However, we have multiple bags of bread bowls taken from the dumpster behind her bakery and from the dumpster behind Cheryl's Seaside Sundries. Forensics is running tests to find out how X15 got into the bread." He continued, "So far, it appears only bags of Thyme Bread Bowls contained the drug. All other bread products from the bakery have come up clean. Receipts from Cheryl's restaurant indicate everyone that became ill ordered soup with that particular bread bowl. Apparently, it's very popular."

Jason nodded in agreement. Dating the baker, he knew how scrumptious her artisan breads were and most everyone in Kill Devil Hills would agree the Thyme Bread Bowls were perfection! The agent continued his debrief. "However, the only bags found at the bakery to have come into contact with the drug were the ones found with Mr. McCallie's body. All others were accounted for at the other lady's restaurant. Right now, we are going on the theory that the drugs were introduced to the breads in transit from the bakery to the restaurant or shortly after arrival."

Cory interjected, "So Logan Jones – Mrs. Maples' nephew – usually delivered the breads, right?" Jason resisted the urge to kick his partner at that moment. They both knew very well that Logan would have nothing to do with drugs. Why his partner was bringing his name up again, he couldn't imagine. Agent Garland nodded, but added that, according to previous testimony, he was not the only one who delivered the breads. Sometimes Krissy Payne picked up the breads on her way into the restaurant in the mornings or in the evenings. She was also the employee responsible for inventorying the breads at night before closing to make sure they had enough for the projected sales the next day. In addition, the young woman had a known relationship with the now deceased drug dealer, Derek McCallie. Jason really didn't like where this was going. Before the conversation went much further, he requested that Cory leave so he could talk to the agent in private for a few minutes. His partner didn't seem too pleased with the request, but left anyway.

"Agent, I think there's some things you need to know before the investigation proceeds," Jason began. Folding his hands under his chin with his elbows propped up on the desk, he nodded for the detective to continue. Jason explained that aside from being Krissy Payne's father, he also had a close relationship with the baker, Mrs. Maples and her nephew Logan. It was hardly a huge revelation. Everyone knew that, including the agent, but he nodded for Jason to continue. The detective explained that he realized his daughter was caught up in the case, but he firmly believed in her innocence. Trying his best not to make the situation worse, he told him about the threatening note Krissy received last night. That information certainly perked the agent's interest.

Thirty minutes later, Jason exited the office feeling a little bit better. The department planned to send an undercover officer to keep an eye on Krissy for her protection. However, she would also need to come back in to file a report for receiving a threat and for more questioning in an effort to determine who could've sent the note. He realized she was still under suspicious for being involved with Derek, now that the DEA was certain he was behind the introduction of illicit drugs into the food supply at Cheryl's Seaside Sundries. Jason left the office with some relief given he felt Krissy would be safer with a cop watching out for her until they could clear up this whole mess.

Krissy arrived at the station with her newly hired attorney, Janice Littleton. Melissa had briefed the attorney on everything that had transpired and everything they knew or suspected up to this point. Even Janice didn't think the situation looked good for the young woman, but there was no solid evidence linking her to the drug or to Derek's death so she was confident things would be resolved quickly. Although nervous about reporting the threat to the cops for fear the culprit would retaliate, the young woman put on a brave face. With guidance from Janice on what to convey during questioning, Krissy explained how Derek had been present at Cheryl's restaurant several nights as she cleaned up before locking up for the night. However, he usually stayed in the back while she tidied up the front counter area. She had also looked the other way when he snuck out a few loaves of bread and some containers of soup since she simply believed he was hungry and had no money to buy food at times. The interview went quickly with the agent instructing Krissy to call him immediately if she received another threat or remembered anything else of importance. On her way out, she kissed her father on the cheek – probably the first time she had done so, since she was ten years old.

Chapter 17

Back at the bakery, Melissa and Logan were cleaning up the mess the DEA had left behind in their search for indications of the X15 drug. A note taped to the counter issued an apology for the mess, as well as an offer to pay for cleaning services. Melissa rolled her eyes and threw the note in the trash. With nothing else to do, with her own restaurant still closed, Cheryl joined her friend at the bakery. They worked together to get the place in working order again. Maddie, Melissa's assistant, had taken the opportunity to visit her grandkids while the bakery was closed but would be back in a couple of days for the re-opening.

Logan had been sent to the local farmer's market for a long list of supplies so the women had the place to themselves for a while. Initially, Cheryl teased Melissa about shacking up with her handsome boyfriend and had been disappointed to hear her friend had moved out at the first opportunity. She knew Jason was head over heels for Melissa. She also knew Melissa still mourned her late husband, but she held out hope that she would embrace a new life and chance at long-lasting love with the right guy. All indications were that Melissa felt the same for Jason, but Cheryl had never heard her mention the word 'love'.

Of course the conversation drifted to the ongoing investigation. Cheryl was anxious to have the whole thing resolved so she could get her restaurant back, but she was fearful that they would discover someone who worked for her was involved. Although the clear front runner for that spot appeared to be Krissy, Cheryl didn't believe that for a second. The girl put forth a tough exterior, but she was highly intelligent and hard-working. Anyone that could quote Shakespeare, Maya Angelou, Walt Whitman, and Edgar Allen Poe as Krissy did on a daily basis, had better things going on in her brain than to allow drugs into her life. Cheryl had found it quite pleasurable listening to the young woman as she delivered trays of food to customers with a smile and a quote for the day. Yes, the choice of Derek as a boyfriend was questionable, but aren't all young girls attracted to the bad boys?

Cheryl asked if the cops had figured out how everyone came to have X15 in their systems since it was highly improbable all the victims were drug users. Melissa answered that it appeared Derek stuffed the bread bowls with small bags of the stuff, but wouldn't someone notice a bag in their bread?

They tossed around a few theories as they continued to clean up when they were surprised by a knock at the front door.

At the door was Dr. Richard Wiggins, the county coroner and Tanner's father, with a load of file folders under his arm. They had gotten to know each other better over the last couple summers as Tanner and Logan became better friends. He was also very well aware of the past troubles they had with the law. He had performed the autopsies on both Linda Stevenson, who was killed inside Melissa's bakery, and Williams Hawkins, who had died of natural causes but it had been suspected he was poisoned by her lemon sage bread.

After a polite greeting, Dr. Wiggins got down to business. He needed Melissa's help. He had run every test he knew to figure out the puzzle how everyone became sick from the drug. It was presumed, after finding the loaves Derek stuffed with bags of the drug, that the drug was consumed somehow. "That's funny," Cheryl interjected, "We were just pondering that same question."

The coroner laid out his files on the counter with a nervous glance towards the front windows. "Neither the DEA nor Chief Monroe would ever condone me consulting a civilian on such a high profile case, but since you made the bread I was hoping we could work together to solve this mystery," he stated. "Without, of course, letting anyone else know." The women readily agreed so the three sat down to peruse his files and brainstorm. All test results indicated the drug had been ingested, but no one would purposefully eat a bag. Cheryl was sure someone would have noticed a bag in their bread and complained.

Melissa asked if he had one of the bags they could examine. Maybe the bags had holes in them or were porous. Dr. Wiggins looked around a little nervously again, so she suggested they adjourn to the back kitchen area where no one could see them from the street. This helped put the doctor at ease. Once the swinging doors closed behind him, he pulled out a flimsy, nearly clear bag. It was entirely too delicate. Not at all like your normal plastic storage bag. It almost had the consistency of cloth. "Do you mind if we run some of our own tests?" Melissa asked. Because he only had the one bag, they agreed to cut the bag into small pieces for the tests.

First, Cheryl held the material over a clear measuring cup as Melissa slowly dripped water onto it. Once the material was soaked, it started to leak water into the cup below. "Interesting," Dr. Wiggins noted. Plastic was not known to become saturated with water at all.

Next, Melissa grabbed a loaf of bread from the refrigerator and defrosted it in the microwave just enough to bring it to room temperature. "Not the most scientific approach, I know," she quipped. Taking a small knife, she cut an incision in the bread and placed a swatch of the material inside. "Cheryl, how hot would you say your soup is when you ladle it into the bread bowls?" she asked. Her friend simply shrugged. "Well, I guess we can do this in small increments and see what happens," Melissa stated as she placed the loaf into the microwave and hit the "30 Seconds" button.

They continued this process for a while. Heating the bread for thirty seconds and then checking the bag. Not much happened except the bag shrunk a bit. Deciding to move on to the next experiment, Melissa repeated the water test with the heated piece of the bag. The result surprised them all. Water immediately flowed through the material. The heat had made the swatch smaller and porous.

The trio ran more tests to see what else affected the consistency of the bag, until they ran out of samples to use. Dr. Wiggins would have to run more scientific tests to show the police in order for it to be used as evidence, but at least they had a working theory. Heat from the soups in the bread bowls caused the bags with the drug to become more permeable than normal plastic bags. The drug would then be able to leach out into the bread bowls and possibly even into the soups. Since most people don't eat the entire bread bowl their soup is served in, perhaps no one consumed the actual bag. Assuming Derek cut miniscule razor slices into the bread bowls, it was possible that the cuts went unnoticed by anyone preparing the bowls, too. At least it was something to go on and it could vindicate everyone that worked for Cheryl, including Krissy.

Chapter 18

Back at Melissa's house later that evening, she filled in Krissy and Logan about the tests conducted on the bread bowls with the bags. The young woman claimed she never saw any slits in the bread bowls, but she also admitted she wasn't that observant when it came to ladling soup into large chunks of bread. Actually, she regretted she had not been there to help with the experiments. Would've been infinitely more interesting than sitting around the house the majority of the afternoon. After her interview with Agent Garland, her new police escort made sure she went straight to Melissa's cottage and stayed there.

The group spent a most welcome uneventful evening of watching Mystery Science Theater and gorging on homemade gourmet caramel and chocolate covered popcorn. Jason called once to check on everyone, but had to stay at work late reviewing the new test results presented by the coroner. Apparently, Agent Garland liked to burn the midnight oil. Jason wasn't sure the man ever left the precinct. He did remark to Melissa that, based on an earlier conversation with the man, the agent seemed highly intrigued by her attorney.

Janice. After a couple comments in front of Cory, Jason decided to fill the agent in on the woman's relationship status before his partner lost his cool.

Cheryl showed up bright and early the next morning with extra-large espressos and cinnamon buns. The two friends relaxed on the back deck while the teenagers slumbered away. Melissa wanted them to get as much sleep as possible. It was probably the first time in weeks anyone had gotten a decent night's sleep. Taking a long sip of the steaming hot liquid, Melissa sighed. "Now this is heaven!" Cheryl eyed her friend suspiciously. Her tense expression did not go along with her statement. Something was bothering Melissa. She hoped to hear that Melissa simply missed living with Jason. When asked teasingly about it, she didn't get the response she wanted.

"Don't get me wrong," Melissa began. "I love Jason, but the last few weeks have been rather stressful. Not exactly the ideal romantic situation. It was rather a relief to get back to my own place." Although disappointed in her answer, Cheryl realized it was exactly what she should have expected.

Seeing that Melissa was not in the mood to discuss her relationship with the delightful detective, Cheryl shifted gears to talk about the ongoing case. She remarked that Krissy's security detail wasn't doing such a great job since he was completely snoozing away in his car when she approached the house. Suddenly she asked, "Hey, have you been able to figure out what Krissy's peek-a-boo tattoo says? After spilling salad all over her trying to get a closer look, it's been killing me not to know." Melissa shook her head. She had completely forgotten about the tattoo.

Krissy soon joined them on the deck. She was wearing pink pajama shorts and a matching tank top. Melissa thought the young woman looked lovely, especially in a color that wasn't black or denim blue which was her usual attire. She almost commented that the pink hue suited her skin tone, but refrained once she realized it would probably cause the girl to run back in to put on something in dreary black. The girl grabbed a cinnamon bun and curled up on the loveseat her father had purchased for Melissa.

After initial "good mornings" were exchanged, an awkward silence followed. Being the more outspoken one, Cheryl decided to bravely ask the big question about Krissy's tattoo. The poor girl turned a shade of pink similar to her pajamas, but she smiled coyly. "Well, see for yourself," she said as she stood up, turned around and tugged the shorts down just a smidgen to reveal the small of her back. Both women laughed when they saw the inscription. It certainly suited the young woman. In beautiful calligraphy were Shakespeare's words from "Hamlet":

"This above all: to thine own self be true."

"That's perfect!" Cheryl cried. Krissy sat back down but pleaded with them not to tell her father. Both held up their right hands and swore silence. They spent the rest of the early morning talking and laughing about everything and nothing. It was a nice change of pace from the tension of the last few weeks. Too bad the good mood was spoiled when Jason called to check in on his girls and to deliver the news that the police and the DEA were no closer to catching up with Derek's X15 contacts then they had been yesterday. After promising to drop by that evening for a family dinner, he ended the call. The smiles were gone off the women's faces. It had been nice to forget about their troubles for a while. Too bad, it couldn't last. They all realized they were no closer to an end to their predicament than before.

Krissy stood up and let out an ear-splitting scream which brought Logan running. Apparently the guard posted for Krissy's protection was either still asleep in his car or simply not doing his job. The young woman paced furiously across the small deck, muttering to herself. Melissa couldn't hear most of what she said, but there were definitely a few select curse words in her ranting. After explaining to Logan that the cops had no new leads which caused Krissy's outburst, Melissa decided it was time to take action herself; her family and friends were at stake. Even though Krissy may not view her as a friend, Melissa cared about her tremendously and knew she would do anything to help the young woman. If someone didn't do something soon, the poor girl could end up paying the price for Derek's malfeasance. "Well, that's just NOT going to happen," she told herself.

Once Krissy stopped pacing, Melissa motioned for the group to move inside to discuss something she didn't want prying ears to hear – especially Krissy's bodyguard. She had a plan to help the cops find the real criminal(s), but she needed everyone's help. For the next couple hours, they hammered out their strategy. First, they had to get by the cop out front without notice. It was decided that Cheryl would leave out the front door. Melissa and Krissy would sneak out the back way and meet up with Cheryl a few blocks over. Logan had to stay behind to cover if the cop decided to check in on Krissy. If he knocked on the door, Logan simply had to report that the girl was still asleep. He doubted the cop would insist on seeing the sleeping teen. However, he wasn't excited about being left behind. Melissa countered that he already had his kicks when he decided to crash the warehouse party without telling her where he was going. This time, he was sidelined.

Chapter 19

The plan worked like a charm. Krissy's bodyguard didn't even notice when Cheryl left the house. He was too busy reading something on his Kindle. Normally, she would be irritated someone wasn't doing their job, especially something as important as guarding someone. However, in this instance, she was grateful. Within fifteen minutes, the other two women joined her and walked the rest of the way to Cheryl's house to get her car. Krissy made a sly comment about Melissa needing to get her own vehicle, but she had gone without one since she arrived back in Kill Devil Hills years ago. She had no plans to purchase one.

Cheryl drove while Krissy navigated to known hangouts and crash pads Derek used during his brief stay in town. They needed to find something to connect him to others dealing or supplying X15. Krissy had the names Tanner got from his buddy, Hoss. She recognized a couple names as being mentioned by Derek at some point in time, but she never met any of them. They checked out half a dozen beach homes that the boy had crashed at when they had been vacant, but all were occupied by vacationers now. They drove by the moving company headquarters in a rundown building on the outskirts of the downtown area. That was when Krissy remembered that Derek had stayed most nights in a room a few floors above the company's office. He had complained that it smelled, had no air conditioning, and only an old mattress on the floor to sleep on. The group decided to check it out.

They parked the car a couple blocks away at a local rental car company. The moving company office appeared abandoned with a sign saying they were out for lunch but would return at 1 p.m. The door was locked so they tried a side door towards the rear of the building. It was locked too. Just as Melissa was about to comment needing Logan's lock picking skills, Krissy took out a hair pin from her ponytail and picked the lock. In seconds, the door swung open revealing a dark corridor. Thankfully, it was also empty.

There were only three floors of the building. They disregarded the main floor since it was clearly utilized just for the moving business. Boxes and bubble wrap filled the tiny hallway. The trio mounted the stairs to the second floor. The odor of burned popcorn and food rotting in trash cans permeated their nostrils. The floor seemed to be a dedicated snack room and hang out area with an old giant box television in the far corner. Krissy cocked her head to the side to indicate they should keep going to the next level.

The third floor was mostly unfinished with rough wood planks for the flooring and an open ceiling that revealed the wires and pipes running throughout the building. One lone fluorescent light hung down in the middle of the hallway. At the end of the corridor was a closed door. All other doorways were minus actual doors. These were packed full of more moving supplies and trash. One small room contained a filthy toilet and small sink that looked as if it had never been introduced to the "scrubbing bubbles". Melissa couldn't believe that Derek lived in these conditions while he was in town. It made her feel sympathy towards him. Perhaps he dealt drugs just to get by.

Krissy didn't need to pick the lock on the door at the end of the hall. It was unlocked. There was trash strewn all over the floor – mostly fast food wrappers and soda cans. Although not in plain sight, they all assumed the place was crawling with roaches and other bugs. There was a dilapidated dresser in the far corner and a lamp missing a lampshade on the floor. There wasn't much to inspect in the room to provide clues to Derek's associates. Krissy checked out the dresser, pausing when she came across his favorite Stone Temple Pilots concert t-shirt and faded blue jeans shoved into a drawer. In the back pocket was a sticky note with the name "Ricky" scrawled on it with a phone number. Krissy recalled that "Ricky" was one of the names of the dealers that Tanner met up with the other night. Well, at least they had a number for him now and could connect him to Derek.

She didn't have time to inform Melissa and Cheryl though before they heard the downstairs metal door bang shut and the sound of footsteps coming up the stairwell. There were only two ways out of the building – those stairs and the fire escape outside the window. Without any place to hide and with the stairs option not viable, Melissa motioned for the others to climb out the window. She nearly had to shove Cheryl outside as the footsteps came closer and closer. Cheryl's fear of heights had the poor woman in a near panic and on the verge of hyperventilating as she looked down through the metal bars of the fire escape landing. Unable to get Cheryl to budge any further, they couldn't escape down the rusty ladder so they ducked under the window sill. Melissa prayed whoever coming down the hall didn't peep outside.

Without attempting to look inside, they heard the door bang open. Whoever was there stomped around loudly. They could hear drawers being opened and thrown to the ground, as well as the lamp crashing against the wall. Krissy stumbled back against the railing when the mattress smashed against the window right above her head. Melissa tried to grab her, but the rusty railing broke from the impact and the young woman fell backwards. Luckily, she grabbed the platform to stop her fall three stories to the ground below. However, the noise alerted the person inside to their presence.

A young man with an acne-scarred face and long greasy hair poked his head out the window to find Krissy dangling from the fire escape and Melissa desperately trying to pull her back up. Cheryl was still frozen in place with a death grip on the railing. The women thought they were goners. Even if this guy wasn't a drug dealer, he wasn't going to take kindly to being caught trashing the place. He started to climb out the window to get to them, but the sudden blaring of police sirens coming down the backstreet stopped him. He hoisted himself back inside and attempted to escape down the stairs. Unfortunately for him, squad cars had already blocked off all exits from the building. Melissa turned her attention back to Krissy's predicament. She vaguely heard a voice over a bull horn instructing Richard "Ricky" Tavales to give himself up peacefully. There was the sound of a scuffle as Ricky tried to bolt out of the building but was tackled by two officers before he could get ten feet away.

Krissy's grip on the platform was slipping fast. Melissa grabbed one of her arms and tried to pull her up. Now was not the time to realize she should have continued regular strength training workouts because her arms were just not up for the challenge. In horror she watched as the young woman lost her hold on the fire escape and plummeted down. Thankfully, her fall was broken by a police squad car that had parked just under them in case Ricky tried to escape that route. The squad car broke her fall. Seeing that the young girl was okay, Melissa almost sighed with relief until she saw the two gentlemen get out of the car. One was DEA Agent Thomas Garland. The other was Krissy's father, Detective Jason Payne. Krissy looked up sheepishly, "Hi, Dad."

Chapter 20

Back at the police station, the two women sat across a small conference table from Agent Garland, Detective Cory Bronson, and Jason. Krissy was in another room having her injuries tended to from the earlier fall from the fire escape. Of the three men, the latter's face revealed the most anger and frustration. Melissa inwardly worried more about what would be said when they were alone outside of this room. Cory had a smug "I told you they were trouble" smile. He seemed as if he were enjoying this situation. While the DEA agent actually looked somewhat amused. Melissa and Cheryl tried their best to appear contrite. No one spoke as they waited for Janice Littleton, their lawyer, to arrive. Even the agent had insisted nothing be said until the attorney could be present for questioning. While they waited, he checked in on the officers questioning Ricky Tavales in another room.

It didn't take Janice long. Melissa had called her earlier that day to inform her of their intentions to track down where Derek had stayed during his time in town, in an effort to find his associates. The attorney had not approved the course of action, but knew better than to attempt talking Melissa out of it. She fully expected to get another call to come to the police station and was prepared. She walked into the conference room with a barely contained smile and slight roll of her eyes in Melissa's direction. "Seems a bit crowded in here, fellas. My clients aren't Al Capone and Bugsy Siegel after all," she began. "Why don't we have Detective Bronson check up on Krissy and then take care of some paperwork or something while we talk?" Cory immediately began to argue, but Agent Garland cut him off by agreeing with Janice and tersely sending him on his way. He earned an appreciative nod and smile from the pretty attorney.

Agent Garland started off by saying, "Okay, ladies, how about you explain what you were doing at the moving company office building and how you managed to be on the fire escape outside the tiny room Derek McCallie formerly occupied?" With a nod from Janice that it was alright to speak up, Melissa explained the whole story. How they had wanted to track down where Derek had been staying in an effort to find out as much as they could about his dealings in town. She also threw in a tiny fib that Krissy needed some closure with Derek's death. Even Jason looked up at her with curiosity at that statement, but he let it slide without question. Melissa told another little lie when she said that the back door of the building was open. No use getting them in more hot water by confessing Krissy picked the lock. She continued to explain what they found, which wasn't much. Melissa fished out the torn paper with the name "Ricky" on it along with a phone number, which Krissy had given to her, from her back pocket and handed it to Agent Garland.

"So is that everything you found, Mrs. Maples?" he asked. She assured him that it was and then explained the rest of the tale. They heard footsteps coming down the hall so they exited via the fire escape in order to avoid any confrontation with someone that may or may not be associated with the drug scene that Derek had been involved in. Cheryl nodded her head in agreement with everything Melissa said. After a moment's silence as the two gentlemen absorbed the information, Agent Garland grinned and started to chuckle. "Ladies, you certainly make things interesting around here." Everyone, including Jason, looked at the federal agent in wonder.

A little while later, Cory walked back in with Krissy in tow. The young woman was bruised, but nothing broken from her fall. Looking sheepishly at her father, she assumed she was in big trouble – not just with the law but with him. Finding the group sitting casually around the conference table and smiling came as a shock. The detective seemed a bit perturbed at the light atmosphere in the room. “Exactly what did I miss?” he asked.

Agent Garland piped up and said the women were free to go and no charges would be filed. He assured the detective they had been reprimanded enough about going off on their own to investigate a crime. However, he did warn Krissy to avoid fire escape ladders from now on.

As the other detective took a seat, the agent continued his explanation. He had hoped Ricky would confess to the murder of Derek McCallie, but the drug dealer had a solid alibi for the night in question – he had been locked up overnight in Nags Head, NC for a DWI (driving while intoxicated). However, he did have some interesting information to impart. Ricky knew all about Derek’s methods of hiding and transporting the drugs. He confiscated bread packages from his girlfriend’s place of employment. He hid the drugs in the bread bowls; however, he mistakenly left a few packages behind one night when his girlfriend finished cleaning up the front of the restaurant early and almost caught him slicing the bread and re-taping the bags. Ricky’s statements cleared Krissy as an accomplice in the drug trafficking. Everyone had been relieved at that news. However, there was still the question of who killed Derek.

Agent Garland surprised everyone when he asked for their cooperation in a plan to entrap the killer. While everyone readily agreed, Detective Bronson wasn't thrilled with the plan and Jason didn't want his daughter involved. Krissy argued with her father. Reluctantly, she showed him the new text she received while she was being evaluated by the medics. It was another threatening note instructing her to keep her mouth shut or else. "I have too much at stake for this to continue, Dad. I'm in this whether you like it or not." He eventually relented after receiving strong reassurances from the agent that she would be thoroughly protected at all times.

Chapter 21

Two days later, Operation Catch the Bad Guy (as coined by Logan) was put into action. Both Logan and Tanner were recruited to help out. Parental permission was necessary. Dr. Wiggins readily agreed, as long as Tanner was protected. Logan's dad had needed a bit more convincing. John David knew his son could take care of himself, as proven over the last two summers with his Aunt Mel. However, he didn't like the idea of intentionally allowing Logan anywhere near known drug dealers. After an hour on the phone with Logan, followed by a half hour with Melissa and Jason together, he gave his consent.

Things had been tense with Melissa and Jason immediately after the episode at the moving company. He really hated that she had taken his daughter in search of Derek McCallie's drug dealing pals. However, Krissy intervened to explain the situation and that Melissa was not to blame. "Come on, Dad! Melissa just realized there was no stopping me from trying to find out the truth so it was better she and Cheryl go with me than let me go alone." Melissa was surprised at Krissy's defense of her, but also delighted. Perhaps there was a chance for them to have a positive relationship after all?

Tanner was pivotal to the plot to unmask Derek's killer. He had the connections and had to be convincing in his role. Neither Melissa nor Jason was certain the young man could pull this off, but he was thoroughly excited at the opportunity to prove himself, especially to Krissy. He spent a lot of time down at the beach hanging with Hoss and his cohorts to re-establish himself as a stoner beach bum. Logan and Emily acted as lookouts. They were always close by, but never made contact with Tanner when he was with the group. Logan liked spending more time with his sweetheart, even if it was in the line of duty. Emily readily accepted the chance to work with Logan to solve a mystery. Although she wasn't Krissy's biggest fan because of the way the young woman treated Logan and his aunt Melissa initially, she appreciated her predicament and gladly offered to help.

Ricky Tavales had readily rolled over on his X15 drug dealing buddies. The cops had the names of at least eight known dealers in Kill Devil Hills. They were holding off making arrests until they could obtain more concrete evidence in the Derek McCallie murder. The eight all worked for the same moving company and were under close surveillance, but that was it for the moment.

It didn't take long before Tanner made casual contact with one of the X15 dealers. The guy had been the one to insist he snort the stuff in front of them last time to prove he wasn't a NARC. They agreed to meet the next day at the fishing pier.

Logan arrived at the pier first, well before dawn even though Tanner wouldn't meet his contact until much later that morning. There were a couple other DEA agents posing as fishermen, too. Logan enjoyed his time reeling in the occasional puffer fish or even a skate, but his nerves were getting the better of him as he waited and waited. His hands shook as he tried to unhook a skate from his line and almost got the wrong end of its barbed tail. Although not poisonous like their stingray counterparts, skate tails have large thorns that can slice up an unwary fisherman. After releasing the creature back into the Atlantic Ocean, Logan took a deep breath to calm his nerves.

Four hours later, Tanner showed up with his Yeti cooler. A couple years ago, the cooler would be full of beer cans poorly disguised as sodas. Although Tanner had stopped this practice recently, for appearance's sake he reverted back to the beer cans. He sat down on a bench just a few yards from Logan.

Neither boy acknowledged the other. Right on time, Tanner's drug dealer contact strolled up and slapped Tanner on the back. Logan inched closer by making it look like he simply decided to change his fishing perch. As instructed by the cops earlier, neither boy looked in the other's direction.

Tanner and his new "friend" made minimal small talk. It was obvious the guy was not comfortable hanging out in such a public place, even if there were only a handful of fisherman on the pier at that time of day. He reached into Tanner's cooler while covertly letting a small bag of powdered X15 fall from his clenched hand into the cooler and then extracting a disguised beer can along with a small plastic bag of cash. Shutting the lid, he immediately made to leave the pier, but Tanner stopped him. "Dude, you've been such a stand-up guy and all, thought I should let you know what I overheard last night when my dad was on the phone with one of his cop pals," he began. That seemed to pique the other boy's interest and he stopped in his tracks. Tanner went on to inform him that the cops had figured out how Derek had distributed the drugs so that everyone got sick. They also had a good idea where Derek got the drugs and that he had been killed because of it. His dad suspected the cops would close in on the suspect later that night. The news certainly rattled the young man.

He thanked Tanner for the tip and immediately rushed away.

True to their recent training in covert operations, Tanner soon left the pier without so much as a glance towards Logan. The other young man continued fishing and whistling to himself. An hour later, Logan packed up his fishing tackle and headed back to his Aunt Mel's house. The undercover agents on the pier texted a picture of the drug dealer to Agent Garland who was waiting with Jason and Cory in an unmarked car a few blocks away. A surveillance unit was put on the boy. He wouldn't make a move without them knowing.

Chapter 22

Later that night, the unit followed the drug dealer back to the moving company building. He went inside the office for a few minutes, but then left in a hurry. Another surveillance crew picked up the trail a block over. They would follow this guy while the original unit stayed behind at the building. Another unit in a SUV with blacked out windows had joined the stake out with a couple civilians in tow – Logan and Tanner. They needed the boys there for a positive identification of the suspect and in case they met up with someone else the boys may recognize. Agent Garland, Jason, and Cory were a couple blocks over as well, waiting on someone to make a move.

A few minutes later, a dark figure exited the building at a fast pace. The person was headed in the same direction as Tanner's drug contact. Logan tried to get a better look at the guy with binoculars, but it was too dark to make an identification. One of the DEA agents handed him another set of binoculars. These had infra-red technology so he could see in the dark. Adjusting the magnification, Logan nearly dropped the binoculars when the face of the man came into focus. The person chasing after the other drug dealer was Kyle Vega. Both Logan and Tanner knew Kyle. They thought he was a really nice guy. He worked at the moving company, so it wasn't unusual for him to be there. Perhaps it was just a coincidence Kyle was leaving so shortly after the drug dealer, and in the same direction. When Logan informed the agents he knew the guy and that the young man's sister was still in the hospital in a coma after accidently ingesting the X15, one of the men radioed the information in. The second surveillance vehicle tailed Kyle just to see where he went, while the other unit stayed behind at the building.

A few minutes later, a call came over the radio informing them that Kyle Vega had indeed caught up to Tanner's drug contact in the back alley behind a local convenience store. Another undercover vehicle pulled up to the building with a handful of squad cars waiting a couple blocks away. The vehicle with Tanner and Logan, as well as Agent's Garland's vehicle, raced off to the store. Nothing good ever happened in back alleys at that time of night. Sure enough, before they reached the store, another call came over the radio for an ambulance. There had been a stabbing.

When they arrived at the scene, Logan and Tanner were instructed to stay in the car – no matter what.

Still not having learned their lesson to obey orders, especially when it came from those in authority, Tanner jumped out of the car with Logan hot on his heels. They were shocked to see the drug dealer being carted off to the ambulance. He was alive, but bloody. Tanner walked into the alley where he witnessed one of the local uniformed cops gently placing a nice-looking, but bloody switchblade into an evidence bag. Looking around, Logan caught a glimpse of Kyle in the back seat of a squad car that had arrived before they did.

The whole story wouldn't come out until much later that night. The drug dealer recovered from his injuries and gave his statement to the police. After informing his dealer buddies at the moving company about the cops closing in on their operation and whoever killed Derek, there had been a huge argument with Kyle who overhead their conversation. He was angry because the X15 they were dealing had made his sister sick. She was still in a coma at the hospital. He knew Derek was behind the drugs getting into the bread, but hadn't known how many of the others were also involved. Kyle had caught up to the dealer in the alleyway and had pulled a switchblade out. Lucky for him, the cops showed up before he received any truly life-threatening wounds.

The more intriguing tale came from Kyle himself back at the precinct. With tears streaming down his face, the young man related a sad, tragic story. While he worked at the moving company, he stayed away from the druggie crowd until his sister became ill. Then he decided to try to find out what he could about the drugs and who was responsible for his sister's coma. It had been easy enough to discover Derek's involvement and he assumed Krissy had been in on the operation too. Kyle swore that he hadn't intended to kill Derek, just scare him into confessing. However, with Derek's confession Kyle only became angrier and couldn't control himself. Before he realized what he had done, Derek was nothing but a bloody, nearly unrecognizable mess.

The young man laid low for a while hoping the cops would pin the death on the rest of the drug dealers or even on Krissy. The more he thought about it, the more Kyle convinced himself that Derek's girlfriend had to know what was going on and had to be held responsible for his sister's condition, too. After getting drunk one night, he snuck into her house to leave the threatening note. When he discovered she'd gone to the cops, but not to confess her own misdeeds (in his viewpoint), he texted her from a disposable phone. He chillingly described how he intended to find her that night and use the switchblade to induce her into confessing. However, he had been sidetracked when he heard the cops were closing in on Derek's killer.

Agent Garland debriefed the entire group around 1 a.m. after getting a full statement from Kyle Vega. The undercover agents that had stayed behind at the moving company office brought in everyone that had been there, and a couple others whose names were already on their watch list based on Ricky Tavales' previous statement. All in all, it had been an eventful and productive night. They had most, if not all, of the X15 dealers downstairs in cells waiting for processing. Kyle Vega would be formally charged in court the next morning for the murder of Derek McCallie, the assault on the drug dealer, and making threats to Krissy Payne. No one would've guessed the quiet young man was capable of such violence. Everyone assumed one of the other dealers or a drug addict had killed Derek. Regardless, the DEA had their drug ring bust and the local cops had their murderer. Best of all, Krissy was cleared of all wrongdoing and could go home with her father.

Chapter 23

The DEA wrapped up their investigation rather quickly after that night. Kyle was sentenced to fifteen years for the murder of Derek McCallie. It was a rather bittersweet outcome as Kyle's little sister Angela emerged from her coma by early August. She had months ahead of her of rehabilitation and physical therapy, but the doctors were optimistic for a full recovery. Sadly, she would face her recovery without her brother by her side to encourage and help her.

Agent Garland successfully utilized the local thugs arrested that night to track down the suppliers. By the end of summer, the national news reported the take down of a major X15 drug ring. Jason and Melissa were watching the press conference when the agent thanked the local Kill Devil Hills police department for help in cracking the case wide open. However, both were shocked when he announced he would be leaving his post with the DEA effective immediately for personal reasons. Jason actually laughed, "Well, that makes sense!" When questioned about it he revealed that his partner, Cory, had been offered a job with the DEA in Miami. According to Jason, the man couldn't wait to get packed up and out of the small seaside community. "Perhaps, Agent Garland doesn't want to work with him again. Cory did follow him around like a lovesick puppy. He talked more about his dream of working for the Feds than the case. I could tell it drove the agent nuts, not to mention Chief Monroe." Melissa admitted Cory wasn't her favorite cop, but she felt sad for Janice. The attorney and detective had been dating for about a year. Then she wondered if perhaps Janice would move to Miami, too. She intended to ask her at the annual end-of-summer picnic at the beach scheduled for the next day.

Everyone was in town for the big summer bash. Logan's mom and dad arrived the night before so the small cottage was bursting at the seams. There was another surprise guest – Melissa's younger brother Jimmy who had been serving several tours in Afghanistan. Their reunion was filled with tears of joy and lots of laughter, as Jimmy was the comedian of the family. Emily's entire family had also been in town for a week, including her brothers who were heading back to college in a couple of weeks.

As Melissa prepared the last of the gourmet burgers for cooking at the beach, she mused how the summer had progressed. Things had started off calmly despite tension from Jason's daughter, Krissy. Melissa had firmly believed she would never get the young woman to accept her in Jason's life, much less actually develop a solid friendship with her. It had been a pleasant, and unexpected, surprise when the turbulence of the summer brought them together.

After all the excitement died down, Melissa and Krissy continued to grow close. The seasoned baker taught Krissy how to cook real meals for herself now that she was going away to college so she wouldn't need to order pizza every night. In turn, the young woman somehow convinced Melissa to color a thick lock of her light auburn hair a deep shade of blue. The women never revealed the true story behind the hair coloring. The two stayed up late one night playing poker and Krissy upped the ante by daring Melissa to color a strand of hair if she lost. Melissa underestimated the young woman's card playing skills and paid the price.

Needless to say, Jason was thrilled to see the two women in his life forging a strong relationship. He broached the subject with his daughter a few nights ago as they went over her checklist for college. She would leave next week for Wilmington and he wanted to ask her opinion on something he planned for the picnic. Krissy's large brown eyes sparkled at what her father was proposing and she readily gave her blessing.

It was a gorgeous day at the beach. Perfect for a large multi-family picnic. Logan and Tanner set up the volleyball net while the adults prepared the food. Tanner kept eyeing Krissy. Never at any point of the summer had she worn a swim suit. She always came to the beach in shorts and tank tops. The young man was hoping she'd break that streak today. He wasn't disappointed. Both Emily and Krissy shimmied off their shorts and t-shirts revealing toned young bodies in somewhat modest bikinis. Tanner and Logan immediately stopped what they were doing to watch. As they ran out into the waves with a couple boogie boards, Jason happened to catch a glimpse of his daughter's tattoo for the first time. He sputtered, "What the ….?" Melissa speedily assured him it was tasteful and not worth scolding the grown woman over. "What? You knew?" he asked. With a sly grin, she simply shrugged and returned to setting out the food.

The day was delightful as family and friends celebrated the end of summer and toasted to lots more summers to come. Cheryl assured Krissy she had a job every year during college breaks, but she declined the kind offer. The young woman claimed that next year she preferred to help Melissa out at the bakery, if she would have her. Surprised, Melissa readily agreed.

Uncle Jimmy had spent the day trying to recruit Tanner into the military. However, he admitted he just wanted to see the kid shave his long locks of hair. Krissy put a stop to that talk by assuring Tanner that she loved his gorgeous blonde mane. To accentuate her point, she walked right up and kissed him on the cheek. Tanner's eyes grew wide as saucers and he blushed redder than any beach sunset. The young man would live off the memory of that chaste kiss until next summer.

As the sun began to set over the famous North Carolina sand dunes, Jason took Melissa's arm in his and strolled away from the others. Despite the brisk wind coming off the ocean, she could instantly tell that the entire group behind them became eerily quiet as they walked towards the pier in the distance. She peeked behind to see every single person watching them. Jason was talking fast, like she knew he did when he was nervous about something. At first he talked of casual topics, like how great the picnic was this year and he enjoyed finally meeting her brother. The two already planned to compete together in the annual Red Drum fishing tournament on Hatteras Island in October. He then moved on to more serious subjects, particularly how happy he was that she and

Krissy were getting along so well. However, he was a little concerned she hadn't told him about the tattoo.

Melissa let him keep talking as they strolled farther down the beach. Eventually, he seemed to run out of things to say and fell silent. Looking back, the large group they left behind appeared as tiny dots on the horizon. Jason stopped just before they reached the pier. This section of the beach was mostly deserted as the vast majority of vacationers had already left town and the regular night fishermen had yet to arrive.

Barely a glimmer of light still shone over the dunes as Jason turned to face his beautiful, sweet, caring girlfriend. There was a knot in her stomach that she couldn't explain. "What is he so antsy about tonight?" she wondered. Melissa didn't have to wait much longer as the handsome detective gathered up his courage. He began by eloquently explaining how the last three summers had been the best time of his life; how she brightened his world each and every day; and how he could no longer imagine his life without her there by his side. Dropping to one knee, Jason pulled out a tiny jewelry box. Melissa's eyes grew wide and her whole body started to tremble as she realized what he was doing. With a shaky voice, he gazed up at his lady love to ask, "Melissa Jones Maples, I love you with all my heart and soul. Never would I have imagined I could feel like this and I don't want this feeling to ever end. Would you do me the honor of being my wife? I promise to spend the entirety of my life making you happy and proving my love to you every single day."

Tears brimmed in both their eyes as Jason waited for her reply. Just a few short years ago, Melissa would never have dreamed she could ever love anyone again as she loved her late husband, Kevin. Jason had never asked her to forget Kevin or the love they shared. He had simply encouraged her to find space in her heart for him as well. She surprised herself when she realized that there was more than enough room for Jason in her heart and in her life. As a single tear slipped down her cheek, she smiled at this wonderful man that had shown her how to love and how to live again. Without a word, her smile grew as she nodded "yes".

Your Free Gift

I wanted to show my appreciation for supporting my work so I've put together a Bonus Chapter for you.

Just visit this link:

http://outerbanksbook3_freegift.gr8.com/

Thanks!

Phoebe T. Eggli

Kill Devil Delicacies' Tantalizing Thyme Bread Bowls

Ingredients:

1 ¼ Cup Water (lukewarm)

2 ½ tsps. Instant Yeast

¼ Cup Oil

3 Cups All-Purpose Flour

½ Cup Semolina Flour

2 Tbsp. Fresh Thyme (finely chopped)

½ tsp Ground Sage

¼ tsp Ground Nutmeg

1 ¼ tsp Salt

1 Tbsp. Sugar

½ Cup Dry Potato Flakes

2 Tbsps. Nonfat Dry Milk

Instructions:

Mix yeast and finely chopped fresh thyme into lukewarm water in a small bowl, then set aside. In a large bowl or mixer combine all dry ingredients first and mix them. Then add the wet ingredients; the oil and yeast and water mixture. Continue to knead or mix until you have a nice smooth dough. Then place in a container where the dough is covered but is allowed to rise for 90 minutes.

After 90 minutes, knead the dough again and separate into six balls and place them on a baking sheet that is lightly greased or lined with parchment paper or a silicon mat. Then allow these dough balls to rise again for 60 minutes. Once risen into nice puff balls, place them in an oven that has been preheated to 350°F and bake for approximately 25 minutes or until they are very golden brown. Then remove them from the oven and allow them to cool, still no the baking sheet. Our goal is to have a nice crusty exterior to hold the soup well!

When ready to serve, cut 1/3 of the bread bowl off the top and pull out the bread on the inside of the bowl. Add your favorite soup and enjoy!

Jalapeno Cheddar Bread

Ingredients:

4 Cups Flour
2 ¼ Cups Water
2 tsp Salt
¼ tsp Dry Active Yeast
2 Jalapeno Peppers seeded and finely diced
(or ¼ Cup Canned Jalapenos finely diced)
1 Cup Sharp Cheddar Cheese – grated
Cornmeal - Sprinkled in the Dutch oven – not mixed in dry the ingredients

Instructions:

Mix flour, salt and yeast in a large mixing bowl. In another bowl add the water and jalapenos and let sit for at least 5 minutes to allow the jalapeno flavor to distribute throughout the water. Then add the water mixture to the dry ingredients. Stir until ingredients are well mixed. Dough may seem extra moist, which is perfectly normal. Then cover the bowl and allow to sit at room temperature for 12-18 hours.

Preheat the oven to 500°F with a cast iron Dutch oven or Le Creuset style enameled pot in the oven preheating as well. Have 1 Cup of grated Sharp Cheddar Cheese ready. Once the oven and Dutch oven has been preheated, pull the Dutch oven out of the oven and remove the lid. Then sprinkle some cornmeal in the bottom of the Dutch oven. On a lightly floured surface pour out the dough, quickly kneed in the grated cheese and form into a ball. Then place the dough inside of the Dutch oven. Replace the Dutch oven lid and place the Dutch oven in the oven. Bake for 30 minutes, then remove the lid and continue to bake for 8-15 minutes, depending on how brown you want the crust to be.

Note: If you don't have 12-18 hours to allow the dough to rest, you may increase the amount of yeast to 1 tsp and only wait 6 hours before baking the dough. However, the longer you wait, the more sourdough-like the bread will be.

The trick to this bread is allowing it to rest for the 12-18 hours and its high moisture content, which turns to steam while being baked with the lid on the Dutch oven. Once we remove the Dutch oven lid, then we begin to bake the outside for a nice crispy crust!

This bread is always a winner! Occasionally, you'll find that one person who doesn't touch jalapenos, but most times everyone leaves raving about how good this bread is!

Kill Devil Delicacies' Bread Sticks

Ingredients:

4 Cups Flour
2 ¼ Cups Water
2 tsp Salt
¼ tsp Dry Active Yeast
Melted butter for dipping bread stick dough prior to baking

Instructions:

Mix flour, yeast and salt in a large mixing bowl. Then add water and mix again thoroughly. Now cover and allow dough to rest for 12-18 hours at room temperature.

Note: If you don't have 12-18 hours to allow the dough to rest, you may increase the amount of yeast to 1 tsp and only wait 6 hours before baking the dough. However, the longer you wait, the more sourdough-like the bread will be.

Preheat oven to 450°F. On floured surface, roll out dough until ½ inch in thickness. Then with a pizza dough slicer, cut dough in 1 inch strips. Take each strip of dough and dip it into the melted butter, then lay on cooking surface, ideally a baking stone, along with other breadsticks. Sprinkle with desired topping and bake for 7-10 minutes.

To add a little flare, you might consider twisting the butter dipped dough a few times before placing it on the cooking surface. Want to get really fancy? Roll in your favorite grated cheese before twisting the bread to make cheesy bread sticks!.

Suggested Toppings:

- Italian Herbs and Parmesan Cheese
- Garlic Powder and Parmesan Cheese
- Cinnamon Sugar
- Chili Powder and Parmesan

First Published, 2015

Timber Publishing
Oakley, UT 84055
www.timberpublishing.com

Made in the USA
San Bernardino, CA
07 December 2015